J. Gennaro Albano is a freelance artist and writer who has lived in Italy for a number of years. *Rome by Night* is one in a series of novels he has written about Italy. Presently, he divides his time between New York and the Eternal City.

Lisa Hope, forever with God and in our hearts

J. Gennaro Albano

Rome by Night

Austin Macauley Publishers™
London · Cambridge · New York · Sharjah

This is a work of fiction; the characters and their names are fictional as are the events. Any resemblance to any person living or dead is coincidental.

Ordering Information
Quantity sales: Special discounts are available on quantity purchases by corporations, associations, and others. For details, contact the publisher at the address below.

Publisher's Cataloging-in-Publication data
Albano, J. Gennaro
Rome by Night

ISBN 9781643786636 (Paperback)
ISBN 9781643786643 (Hardback)
ISBN 9781645364795 (ePub e-book)

Library of Congress Control Number: 2020909724

www.austinmacauley.com/us

First Published (2020)
Austin Macauley Publishers LLC
40 Wall Street, 28th Floor
New York, NY 10005
USA

mail-usa@austinmacauley.com
+1 (646) 5125767

Part One

Rome by Night

"…Where anything can happen in secret and usually does and hits the headlines next morning."

Gianni Fascati, paparazzo and freelance photographer

Vespers...

Un canto... a solemn song vibrating a melancholy from the car radio, along the via of ages, in a night surrendering to a full candid moon; lingering above the Forum pilasters and columns casting ancient shadows dissipating slowly in Rome by night, *'La romana'* dancing in the silhouettes of cypress that shoulder the road legions once took, stopped and surrendered to a smile. "Gianni sei tu."

As the radio played another memory, she went over to her pink Fiat Spider convertible that clients never failed to recognize, leaned over exposing strong legs under a pink mini skirt, and reached into the back seat to pull out a small wood box and came to him.

"Sabine! What is left of her are her ashes. Take them and do with them as you promised you would. Keep Annabelle in mind, if you want to find out about Sabine!"

He placed the box behind the driver seat of his white Maserati "Gran Turismo" convertible and sped off from the park.

Night Calls

As the building porter peered from the cubical window, the light from the desk lamp reflected off his face; when he looked up, he recognized Gianni, who passed quickly and ran up the stairs to the first landing. He knocked hard against the door of the apartment that he knew well, then rang the bell, and waited no more than a few seconds, then struck repeatedly at the door again till it opened with the sound of light laughter and then Annabelle in a towel. She nervously tugged at the towel around her breasts as her laughter disappeared into surprise and a caustic demand. "Oh you! Why are you here?"

"To see you, Annabelle! No offer of a cup of coffee?"

She glared at him with darkening eyes and brushed wet black curls of hair from her face, and then surrendered, "You know where it is, make it yourself!" She turned quickly without looking at him to run down the hallway to the bathroom, the towel separating in stride around the soft under-curve of her firm bum. He decided on a hard drink instead of coffee and went to the sitting room. The room had the look of a woman now that she had removed everything that referenced him, except for the piece of art on the wall above the cabinet that he now searched for a drink. He knelt down on both knees and explored the stash and settled on brandy, took a long glass from the shelf near the kitchen doorway, cleaned it of dust with a napkin that was on the shelf, poured it half-full, and sat down on the satin upholstered sofa, and rested his feet on the glass covering of an expensive coffee table.

As he drank, his eyes settled on the large photo print above the cabinet from the series he did of Estelle for the Milan show. He stood and went closer to study it till Annabelle's voice caused him to turn, "Estelle…your model…your slut; tell me did shagging her improve your art as you like to call it."

She was wearing a bathrobe and shook her hair by moving her head and stroking it as an ironic smile crossed her lips.

Gianni glared back, "No more than you did."

"I see you can't keep off the hard stuff."

"Just a drink to celebrate how well you are doing without me. Have one and we can celebrate together. Sabine told me that Leonardo treats you well!"

"Sabine! Were they the last words from her mouth before she died?"

"I think you might know what her last words were. I think you know a lot that I don't know about Sabine and her escort business," he moved towards her.

"You've had your drink, now get out!" she moved to the door and opened it, "Get out or I'll ring the police."

"Ring the police or shall I?"

She slammed the door, then came to him, "What do you want?"

"You're trying to pin her murder on me by feeding misinformation around the cabaret and to the police about my relationship with her!"

She went to the sofa, sat and took a cigarette from a pack on the coffee table, lit it, and sat back to smoke as the opening to her robe fell away and exposed much of her breasts, "You were shagging Sabine. I wasn't, for the Rome police that would be enough for probable cause. You know how they are here. Sabine being found dead in the Tiber and the story about you and her was floating around, pardon the pun, it all leads to you. The way the police see it, it is a case of 'love gone wrong,' and that compliments their desire to wrap up a sordid murder case quickly. I only confirmed what the police already knew about the two of you."

"I wasn't shagging her, as you put it!"

She burst into laughter as she put a leg on the coffee table, causing the opening of her robe to expose more of her nude body. When she noticed his sudden unease at her nudity, she pulled her robe open and smiled, "Seems you still are affected by something from the past that you cannot have anymore."

He lunged at her and called out, "You're a bitch!" and grabbed her robe and pulled her to her feet crushing her against him.

"Are you going to choke me to death like you did to Sabine?" she glared into his eyes, "This is more emotion than you've ever shown in bed!"

He pushed her down onto the sofa, "I never touched Sabine! And you're a gypsy bitch and you belong working the back streets with the rest of Rome's hustlers! That's what you were doing in Naples, wasn't it, when you ran up to my car? Hustling on the waterfront and being chased by a guy you rolled and his friends. I should have left you to them, instead of picking you up and saving you.

"Sabine told me that you worked at her escort enterprise. She told me about you and Leonardo and about her little black book of names with information in it. Bad stuff about big shots in Rome. Rich guys, perverted politicians with under-age girls, and if the news media got the information, it would bring down the government. It would bring down your dear Leonardo, wouldn't it?"

Annabelle's eyes flashed at him with hate, "You killed her for the book with the list of names, didn't you!"

He turned and went to the door, opened it, and glared back at her, "Did I? How did you know Sabine was choked? The police have not released a cause of death!"

He slammed the door behind him when he left.

The reflection of blue neon from the 'Cabaret Rome by Nite' splashed on the charred night walls and ran along a side street and onto the narrow sidewalk like a run off seeking the front fender and hood of a parked white Maserati convertible with the driver side tires flagrantly violating the small sidewalk. The loneliness of the side street explained itself in the empty echoes of distant laughter from a tart hustling a drunken mark and the muffled hum of the nightly motorcade, along the Via Veneto a short walk from the nightclub entrance, where a slim figure in a black jacket and porter cap acted as doorman who recognized the lean figure exiting the white convertible and approaching the cabaret entrance and saluted him by tipping his cap, then opened the plated glass door of the cabaret entrance for him, and watched him disappear inside the cabaret show-room where showgirls danced to an erotic beat.

Gianni hesitated for a moment as he searched the cabaret for the owner. Then he moved deliberately toward a booth where the owner sat alone enjoying a cigarette and brandy in the semi-dark interrupted by the colored gels' overflow from spotlights focused on the showgirls performing on the dance floor. He was bald and small wearing a 'Night' jacket over worn black pants, black tie, and white shirt. A Turkish cigarette stuck to the corner of his broad and parched lips. Friends and clients knew him as Elio, the Egyptian. His dark eyes stammered as they focused on the showgirls and then on the slim figure in his late twenties approaching him who was middle-sized and wore a worn brown sport jacket over a light gray pull over and jeans and was always clean-shaven with groomed wavy dark hair that complemented Mediterranean eyes and an easy smile that attracted showgirls.

Elio smiled, "So, then, Gianni sit. I knew you would come. It was just a matter of time. What are you drinking?"

"Whatever you're having."

The Egyptian motioned to a waitress who was wearing a bold blue costume cut to reveal much of her breasts and legs. She smiled at Gianni when she came to the booth and leaned toward him as he gave her a kiss on her cheek. Elio showed his glass to her and pointed to his younger friend then sent her off with a glance towards the bar.

"You have a weakness for pretty showgirls and waitresses with nice breasts, Gianni. Be careful, my boy, body parts lead to trouble. I've told you that before…am I not right? Showgirls bring problems, first Annabelle and then that thing with Estelle that broke things up for you with Annabelle and your relations with poor late Sabine… Look at the mess you are in now because of her."

As Elio waited for a reply the music stopped, then some scattered applause, and suddenly a tall blond appeared in her showgirl costume, the top cut away enough to expose most of her breasts, while the bottom was a net mesh brief with a high-cut at her hips that made her long shapely legs seem even longer.

"Talking business and not minding my lead performance in the chorus, I'm sure." She had a public-school accent of the privileged class of England and the trained manner of being polite in any conversation.

"Of course not, Estelle, we always talk of your talents darling," Gianni replied with an affectionate smile.

"Which ones, Nit?" She brushed a blond wave of hair from her face and kissed him leaving a red violet smudge on his cheek and then sprang away, "I'm off for costume change for the next number; see you tonight, darling?"

"Of course!" Gianni replied with a soft smile.

The showgirl smiled back, then ran off as the waitress returned with his drink, gave him a quick smile, and moved away when Elio leaned across the table, "Now, that Estelle has gone, what really happened between you and Sabine, and my dear American friend, please, for your sake, be truthful."

"How bad is it, Elio?" the American whispered.

The cabaret owner took the cigarette from his mouth and crushed it into the ashtray at his wrist, "The police have you down as the last to see Sabine alive. That is why they are investigating you. Interpol has information on you about the strange death years ago of a stripper in Brooklyn. She died a few months after she was found in a drug coma in the same loft where you lay unconscious do to a wound over your eye that was the result of a bullet targeted to kill you. The scar is still quite noticeable, you know. Gives you an accent of the sinister that I am sure appealed to Sabine, who, also, was found dead and who happened also to be a stripper. It would appear that association with you by strippers is a dangerous venture. That is what the police think according to my informers. But the police are not your real problem. With them, you can only do time. It is the others, my friend that you must fear. So, have your drink and let's hear the story about Sabine and the last time you saw her alive and then I will see if I can help," Elio's glare challenged the American's nervous eyes.

The American took a drink, then placed the glass down deliberately, and focused his stare at the cabaret owner, "It was two days before she went missing. I needed a model for a location shoot on the coast when a model canceled at the last moment. I used Sabine before for beach shoots; she had the Mediterranean look and the developed body for swimwear. I knew she was hard up after you fired her and no one would hire her because she was under investigation for running a bordello with teen escorts. So, to survive, she took to the streets. I met her at a small café off the Tiber, where I was told she hung out and met clients and offered her to come with me to Positano on the coast for the swimwear magazine shoot. She agreed only if I paid her extra for the loss of clients she would have. I agreed because I needed someone right away. She made me take the picture of her posing as a street walker in front of the street poster outside the café before we left that the newspapers and T.V. got a hold of…"

Elio jolted back in his seat and interrupted him, "And caused the whole story to be sensationalized. And targeted you in the eyes of the police. How ironic, with all the traveling you have done as photographer and paparazzo over the years taking thousands of photos of women to get the one photo that could make you famous and rich and then you take one by circumstance and it implicates you in a scandal when it gets leaked to the media and endangers your life."

Elio seized Gianni's arm, "Yes, endangers your life, because the photo connects you to her and her bordello; and word is that Sabine kept a book with her clients' names, dates, money transactions, and information about important clients in the government. The scandal of all those very prominent names… Politicians in the highest offices of this government frequenting a bordello of under-age girls run by Sabine, who was found lifeless floating in the Tiber, would bring down the government.

"It seems she was killed to keep her quiet and get the book and the police believe her murderer has it. They think that you know everything about her illicit business and that you have the book and you were the last to see her alive according to them and that makes you suspect numero uno."

Gianni freed his arm, "The murderer was the last to see her alive, not me. I know nothing about her escort operation and a book and the names, other than what she told me at my other studio in Pompeii when we came back from the beach and finished the shoot. She said she had a little black book with information that was connected to her escort business. She said the book would get her off. But I have no idea where it is. That's what I told the police."

The Egyptian was silent as he studied the American, then he took another Turkish brown from a silver cigarette case, and tapped it as if to pace his thoughts, "Don't lie, the police are not your only problem, my friend. The stakes are life and death… I can assure you there are people who will stop at nothing to get the book!" With the final word, he lit the cigarette with a lighter that had diamond chips encrusted on the face.

"I know nothing about the book other than what she said."

Gianni focused on the figure before him who always called him "my American friend" but realized that the years he had known him as a friend mattered little now.

Elio drew a thought with the smoke of the cigarette, "I have contacts in the magistrate's office, expensive contacts who inform me at a great price to keep me informed, that there is a script taken from your studio called Rome by Night. The title gives me alarm and inclines me to believe that it is about me in one way or other…at minimum this place and things that go on behind the scenes or as you call them, in America, under the radar, and combined with the scandal that Sabine was involved in while working here, brings a lot of unwanted attention to this place and to me. And I hear that you and Sabine were working on this script together…"

Gianni interrupted him; "The idea for the title came from this place true but just the title. Sabine used it for the script treatment, it was a treatment not a full script, just ideas we collaborated on a while back when she was working on a production at Cinecittà studios and doing some script editing. She did some acting and modeling as well. You know that when she first started here, she worked here at night stripping and at the studios and was a 'four o'clock girl' for producers as well. How do you think she got all those celebrity and political contacts for her own escort enterprise?"

Elio leaned forward to whisper, "Enterprise… We are beyond enterprise here! Sabine was a madam for under-age girl escorts with a client list that reaches celebrities and high-ranking politicians of this government and in the middle of the investigation, she is found floating down the Tiber. My informants tell me that the cause of death is being held secret by the police in order to entrap suspects, I am sure, but they were able to find out that tap water, not Tiber water, was found in her lungs. Evidently, a form of inquisition by water was applied to try and get information, a method popular in your adopted America by the CIA known as water boarding, raising suspicions about you, my naturalized American friend. Are you a CIA operative?" He smiled, and then took a drink from his glass of brandy.

"I know nothing about how she died or was murdered! And I don't know a damn thing about water boarding!"

The Egyptian leaned closer to him and whispered more softly, "Perhaps not, but I believe you know about the names and the much sort after book! It will be in your interest to cooperate with me I assure you. Don't you see if you hold onto the book, the killer will be after you? Give it to the police and it benefits no one and brings harm to many respected and powerful men… Give it to me and there is profit. Great profit for us both, my young friend.

"You are a target now with the book. Even if you bring it to the police, they will target you as an accomplice to her enterprise, as you call it. And they will use it as evidence in a murder indictment against you. You know how the magistrates are here in Italy. They will want to get an easy scapegoat, as you Americans call it, and cover up for the rich and powerful; I know the narrative and it will be in the media the next day when they arrest you. Lovers' quarrel, a crime of passion, and you killed poor Sabine, or you killed her to shut her up because she was going to tell all to the investigating magistrate and implicate you. They will create the story and they will convict you!"

Gianni protested, "I have no list of names and no black book!"

"And the script, my contacts say there is a copy found and the police are investigating it to see if it is evidence," Elio pressed him.

"Right… she kept a copy in my studio and the police took it when they searched it. It is a story about her, about her life living in the shadows of society…in Rome by night, as she phrased it. She compared her life as a modern escort to the life of the courtesans in Renaissance Rome."

The Egyptian interrupted, "Are you sure there are no names in it? References…descriptions of certain characters resembling people who wouldn't want to be characterized?"

Gianni shrugged, "If she added to it, I don't know. What I saw back then was a scene treatment outline; a bunch of ideas. That's it. We were supposed to collaborate on a script, but we never did."

Elio leaned back and nursed the cigarette, then took a pensive drag, exhaled, and asked "Tell me about it. Can you? And try and recall everything, my dear friend."

Gianni thought for a moment as he looked on the dance floor where Estelle came out to perform her 'Mask' dance and then he turned to Elio, and recalled, "Sabine wanted to do preliminary shooting and also work on the script with me. She knew that I had done a couple of documentaries and had video equipment at the studio. She wanted to do a promo clip with her in the lead role and bring it to a producer she was running around with who had connections at the Cinecittà studios.

"She developed the storyline about a courtesan in Renaissance Rome, who modeled for, both, Michelangelo and Raffaello. An over-the-top kind of thing, I felt, but it had some attractive elements. She used the Renaissance costumes I had at the time from a fashion video I did for a Paris house. I used her as a model in it. She dressed as a courtesan in the scenes we did for her film. And then we were to develop the modern-day scenes together based on her escort enterprise in Rome by night, which, according to her, was the evolution of the Renaissance courtesan's life-style. It was all about two women in two periods of Rome by night, both trying to survive in different times, the courtesan back then and the escort today.

"When we came back from that last beach shoot in Positano, we did additional swimsuit photography for it at my studio in Rome. After we finished, we had some wine and snacks and she told me she was still working on the script. She said she was comparing a courtesan in the Sixteenth Century and the men who paid for sex and kept her until they all abandoned her with what she was experiencing, because of the modern Roman men who abandoned her. She told me she awakes crying and promises to get vengeance on all those prominent Romans who have forced her into the streets, instead of protecting her…"

"So, there it is!" Elio's voice silenced Gianni, "She wanted vengeance against important Romans. I am always amazed how in Europe women are so much at the center of things. Men are so much more the fools here than in the Middle East when it comes to women. Look at the mess this little French tart Sabine has caused. A woman like her would have been dealt with in Egypt long before she could do tragic damage."

Gianni finished his glass of cognac and was attracted to the stage where Estelle performed her sensual dance and replied pensively to the Egyptian, "Tragic damage wrapped up in a package of sensual beauty for men in Rome by night."

The Egyptian noticed Gianni's distraction for Estelle's performance, "Tragedy, my young friend, is to be a fool about beautiful women in Rome and anywhere else in the world. Don't be one. Especially, now, because Sabine's death has put you in danger. The black book is your death warrant. Be smart and tell me the truth about what she told you about it." The Egyptian leaned closer to him and spoke, "I can help you, if I get the book, I know what to do with it and instead of it being a source of danger for you, it will be treasure for us both. You must understand. The book is worth a fortune to certain people."

"The problem Elio is I have no idea where it is!" the American turned and stared at him.

"I am no fool!" The Egyptian leaned back, "I don't believe you. I know about your past in Brooklyn…"

"Don't bring that up!" Gianni glared at the Egyptian.

"Calm yourself, I am your friend. I mean nothing by that but your friends in Brooklyn would also be interested in the black book, no? And as always, I am here to make a deal with anyone." He studied Gianni, who looked again at Estelle's performance, "Think of Estelle, my friend, and what the two of you could do with all the money the black book would bring."

The Trastevere quarter of Rome by night embraced the solitude of a medieval cloister; the walls, charred with the sediment of time, echoed the night's sinister footfalls of strangers risking the dark labyrinth of ancient passageways and the roar of the white Maserati, lapping dark foreboding shadows as it sped along the Lungotevere drive at the edge of the Tiber in pursuit of a mystery and being followed at tailing distance by a black Alfa Romeo sedan.

Estelle's small apartment was in a worn walk up in a tight alleyway that interlocked into the maze of ancient passages that twisted along the Tiber River. It was past two when she arrived tired from the last cabaret performance and woke him as he slept on the couch in the sitting room part of the one-bedroom apartment. She made coffee and they sat in the small area that served as a kitchen with a small table and a pair of worn wooden chairs placed under a small skylight that gave the space air and light. The conversation fell immediately on Annabelle.

"Do you believe she had anything to do with Sabine's death?" Estelle's voice gave no indication of alarm, as her eyes searched his for a suggestion of suspicion.

"I have information that the police are not going to release the cause of death yet. But Annabelle said that Sabine was choked."

"Maybe it was just an assumption on her part," the casualness of Estelle's remark suggested a disinterest in Annabelle.

"Maybe?" he stood up and went to the couch again to stretch out.

She came over and stood over him, "Let's talk about you and forget about Annabelle. I know how Sabine's death affected you. Elio warned me about you tonight. He said that you are a marked man now and mentioned you had trouble in the past in Brooklyn. He also said that being investigated by the police is not your only trouble. Then he walked away without another word. Tell me what is all this about. Tell me the truth now!"

She sat beside him after he moved to let her, and then embraced her. But she shifted from him and asked coldly, "What is happening Gianni, please tell me the truth."

He studied her for a moment and saw the determination for the truth in her eyes and then began to talk deliberately and cautiously as he explored the past to try and find sense in what was happening to him. " You, the police, Elio… everybody has it wrong about me and Sabine. We were never really an item. There were moments we were together but brief. We weren't a good match. I was too much a traveler…"

"Still are Nit," Estelle cut off his thought, "Will be forever, it's in your blood. I think of you as a prowler, like an alley cat or perhaps more kindly a traveler by night. Yes, that's it, a traveler by night wandering about in the dark not knowing where it will all lead to. Am I not right, Gianni?"

He ignored the question and recaptured his thoughts,

"Sabine had a discipline about her…"

"A bitch! A real one backstage," the angry words came out with the burst of smoke from Estelle's lips after lighting a cigarette, "Go on then, sorry, didn't mean to interrupt, I lose a bit when I think of working with her, sorry again."

He reached over to her and took the cigarette from her hand and took a long drag and nursed the smoke as he recalled the past again and she lit another cigarette for herself and settled beside him to listen.

His mind searched for the details to tell her, "The last time I saw her was when I needed her for the time of the essence assignment for beachwear for a magazine spread. I did the studio shoot at my place near Pompeii and used the nearby beach for the beach scenes, and then we went to Positano for location shoots in the town. Sabine had never seen the Amalfi coast and was taken by the beauty and it seemed to lift her spirits. I mentioned that I grew up in the area and she remarked that I was lucky to grow up in such a beautiful place.

"We had dinner at a hotel restaurant and took a table on the *terrazzo*, overlooking the town and the beach and I pointed out the hill where I fell into an ancient grave when I was a kid playing soccer. I had chased the ball off the field and the ground gave way and I fell in. My mates ran over and dug me out, but as I was digging to clear my legs, I felt something. It turned out to be a body wrapped in rotted cloth. Everyone started to grab it and the cloth fell apart and the body it contained disintegrated into a pile of dust that a strong wind dispersed over the field and out beyond the mountains and over the sea.

"We later found out that the grave was ancient when archeologists from Naples came to examine it. The grave was of a young woman they said, because of the bracelet they found when they excavated. She may have been a servant girl or slave. Sabine said that the girl was probably a sex-slave used by Roman men, and ancient times or modern times things stay the same. Then she said that it was a good thing that the young slave girl's remains were liberated to the beauty of the place and that she would like that for her ashes when she died. She kissed me and asked me to remember what she said."

"Remember what she said? It seems she had thoughts about death. Suicide, wouldn't you think, Nit? Don't you see, darling, she sounded completely suicidal. Did you tell the police this?"

"The investigating magistrate was indifferent to it."

"Is there more to the story?"

"We drove back to my other studio near Pompeii. We drank a great deal…"

"And shagged!" she glared at him.

"Believe it or not, no."

"I don't believe you!" she looked away.

"You never have!" he responded flatly.

"Then what happened?" she looked at him again.

He returned her glance and continued, "Sabine was lit up with a lot of wine setting off her bitchy side…"

"She didn't need wine for that, especially, backstage!" she brushed a wave of blond hair from her eye.

He continued after the outburst, "She started in with me, 'you are somber tonight. I see that Annabelle affects still and that you are a fool about women as all men are who bother about them. The one thing that bothering men don't understand about their women is that their women always win.' She told me that Annabelle would work at her enterprise, as she called it, when she felt like it, when I was away on assignments until she hooked up with Leonardo and stopped just in time to avoid the scandal and Sabine ended up in the small café off the Tiber, too toxic to bother with even by pimps.

"She was angry at being deserted by everyone, especially powerful people, who could have helped her but didn't. She told me she had all the important client names recorded in her little black book with little notations and other evidence safe with her, until it was time to reveal the truth and get back at them."

"How long did you stay in Pompeii?"

"Two days."

"Did she bring things with her?"

Gianni paused before he answered and studied her, "Like what?"

"A change, an overnight?" Estelle pressed as she looked into his eyes.

He looked away and answered, "She had a bag that was always with her and didn't bother getting anything else. She could wear things that I had stored from previous shoots. So, she didn't need to bring much. Why?"

“Did you tell the police this?” Estelle stood and glared at him.

“They didn’t ask me. What are you getting at?” he looked at her again.

“Sabine was a meticulous dresser. I find it strange she would leave and not bring things with her. She leaves with you on the trip to the coast for two days and brings nothing with her but a handbag and then she is found dead in the Tiber a few days later. It doesn’t look good, Gianni. Elio warned me that you are not only mixed up in this Sabine mess, but you also have a dangerous past in Brooklyn.”

She passed a hand over the scar over his right eyebrow. “You said you got this in Brooklyn. The result of a bullet meant to kill you and never talked to me about it again. Should I be afraid of you?” Estelle fell into a silence that recalled British school propriety and very unlike the clatter of the Neapolitan women he grew up with.

He studied her and saw the concern in her blue eyes, “Perhaps you should be afraid and Elio is right. Perhaps, Sabine should have been afraid as well. What happened to me in Brooklyn may be a part of this. I haven’t sordid it out. I was wrong to come here tonight. Things are too hot. I learned tonight that I might have more to fear from Elio than I have to fear from the police.”

He reached the Maserati when the early morning sky chased the shadows, along the Lungotevere drive, and traffic began to rise in pursuit of another workday. As his convertible made its way toward Monte Mario, he saw a black Alfa Romeo in the rear-view mirror deliberately scale the sidewalk with the driver side tires to pass a small truck that was laboring with a heavy morning-load along the drive and he knew that he was being followed.

His place was a loft on the first landing in an office building off the Lungotevere drive. It was a large space that was used years ago as a printing studio. He used the place for photography and video recording as well. He created a bedroom space with a bath separated by a wall he built himself from the studio set area and a small sitting-area. There was a kitchen space near a large window that overlooked the Lungotevere road and the Tiber River. As he lay in bed, he looked at the small box with Sabine's ashes he had placed on the wall shelf in the bedroom area. He tried to put the scattered pieces of information together that would solve the mystery of who killed her and if what happened in New York on the Brooklyn waterfront, five years before, had anything to do with the danger he faced now from Elio and the police and others. When sleep came, it brought a recurring dream from the past in Brooklyn.

The Hit

A man seen through an open bathroom doorway shaving; an old song on the radio in English; Old Spice after-shave on his face, then washing his hands; a fade to the man moving into the kitchen taking his shirt off a kitchen table chair, putting it on, and then a tan sport jacket hanging on a closet door, shutting off the radio and going out the door into the tenement hallway and finding the stairs and running down quickly while whistling the tune from the radio.

Opening the inner lobby door, suddenly a long muzzle of a pistol with a silencer touching his chest and a small flash and a popping *thud* sound… Everything to black and then a second popping *thud* sound…

In the dark interior of a funeral chapel, two women in black sitting next to an open casket; the New York Post newspaper with a headline 'Brooklyn Waterfront Rubout' on a table next to them.

Then the waterfront at night and a ship at the dock, an officer waving on the bridge, black smoke bellowing from the smokestack, a ship horn sounding in a dense fog, and a sound of gunfire mixing with the wailing of police sirens…

Suddenly, a flash of light and a hand on his chest…

Scattered Takes

Gianni awoke to find Jill leaning over him and whispering in his ear, "Thought you were dead, darling!"

He sat up and tried to clear his head and cried out, "Turn the damn light off, damn you!"

"My…my darling Gianni gets angry as a baby when awakened. Estelle never mentioned it to me. Then I must remember; never disturb baby darling from sleep," she laughed then slipped her light blue shift dress over her blond hair and threw it toward a chair, then pushed him back on the bed, and threw a leg over his body and forced her large naked breasts into his face, leaned into him and kissed him and then whispered, "Let's shag a bit before work darling Gianni!" as her long blond hair cascaded over his head and shoulders.

He turned quickly and flipped her over, seized her hands and crushed her as he vaulted on top of her, "Where's the dust! The snow, you dumb English tart."

She laughed, "Tart, is it! Yes, tart then take me, now!"

He came to his feet, looked around the room, and found her summer shift thrown over the back of the chair with her white lace brief on the seat, then he saw her bag at the feet of the chair, and went for it. He picked it up as she jumped from the bed and screamed and rushed to him.

"No! What are you doing, you dumb bastard!"

He side stepped her and ran into the kitchen area as she chased him without bothering to put anything on and caught up with him at the sink, as he turned the open bag and let fall its contents into the sink. He shoved her to the ground when she grabbed for the contents and then turned on both faucet taps drowning the fallen objects.

"You dumb fool!" she screamed, as she came to her feet and attacked him. But he held her off and pushed her down again, turned, and put both hands into the flooding sink and finally fished out a cellophane packet, held it above his head as she came to her feet again, crying, "No, please, Gianni, let me have it, I'll be good to you forever… Look at me, you love my body… I see it in every shoot! You want my body… I see it now in your eyes as I have always seen it… The showgirl body they love at Elio's cabaret…as you like it now, darling!

"Give it to me!" she reached for the packet as he ripped it open and the white powder fell into the sink water. When she jumped onto his back, she grabbed the packet, but it was too late and she ran off to the bedroom-space with it and licked the remnants of the powder and then threw herself on the bed and cried.

She was still sleeping an hour later when he came to the bedroom-space with coffee, so he returned it to the small table in the kitchen and finished the breakfast he had made of coffee and bread with peach marmalade and left some for Jill. After he cleaned up, he went to the window in the kitchen-space, looked out, and saw the black Alfa on the far end of the small pocket piazza. Suddenly, he felt Jill's warm body lean into his back, "Been a bad girl, darling, forgive me."

She kissed his neck and then his lips when he turned and embraced her naked body.

"You have costumes sectioned out on the rack for the shoot," he said forcefully.

"We have the shoot, yes, darling," she smiled softly and stepped away to the window.

"I set up everything for the shoot while you slept. Are you settled enough?"

"Of course…the stuff is recreational, helps me relax… I went right off and then up in an hour, as you can see, ready for work now."

"The stuff as you call it killed my brother and got me this crease over my eye in Brooklyn." he went to her as she looked out the window and fit an arm around her waist to draw her warm naked body to him.

She placed a soft hand on his arm and glared at the river across the street, "You told me about Brooklyn before, dark things then, darling, and now, Sabine. They say she was found in the river near your place here. Is that true, darling?"

"Yes."

She turned to him to study his expression, and then turned and looked out the window again, "It was cold that night when it happened, I am sure. It's Rome and English people think it is warm or hot all the time, but it really isn't that way. It can get cold. There's always a chill at two in the morning after the last show when I used to leave the cabaret. It always gives me a bit of a shake, you know, slight quick body tremors as my legs feel the chill but then gone quickly.

But the water, the murky-shit floating down there is a different thing, don't you think, darling?" She turned and leaned into him, then put both arms around his waist, and he felt her warm naked body perspiring.

"Things are bad all round after Sabine's death, you see. I worked for her at her little enterprise. And now Elio sacked me, because he found out I was using. I need this work now and the money. Sabine's cash made life comfortable; supplementing the cabaret pay but now all that's gone."

The soft afternoon light from the skylight window made her face look natural. She took a drag from her cigarette and then placed it in the side of her lips and let the smoke escape, while she adjusted the string top of a green floral bikini and then the small brief as she stood before the white screen in the set up for Gianni's Leica studio camera.

"How did you get in?" Gianni asked, as he adjusted the camera lens.

"Vincenzo, the palazzo portiere, heard me pounding on your door and took the opportunity to assist the English showgirl he so much admires, especially semi-nude on stage at the Cabaret Rome by Nite, where he is genially treated, and always satisfied with a smile and a kiss on the cheek from this sensual blond showgirl, as most middle age Italian men are."

"You should know."

"I do know about the usual type, the harmless ones. It is the rich and famous ones that one has to watch out for. The ones in dark gray Armani suits with gold ties and monogrammed silk shirts and sweet Gucci cologne and manicured nails and hard hands."

"The type at Sabine's enterprise."

She posed for the camera lens giving him opportunity to focus her. "The types who came to Sabine's enterprise, yes! Yes, the dear honorable *signori*! I have had my time with them." She laughed ironically and turned her head to the left to greet an imaginary client and act out a surprise, touching her cheek with the hand that held the cigarette, then with the other hand, pulling the string of the Bikini top and letting it fall exposing her breasts, "Oh! Oh, my dear honorable senator, excuse me…"

She laughed again and puckered her lips, turned her head, and cat-walked to the camera lens and kissed it then walked away toward the dressing area and called back to him playfully, "Did you like that, darling?"

He stepped away from the camera, cleaned the lens with a cloth and marked a spot for her on the set and then advanced toward her, as she turned to him and took a long drag and exhaled the smoke when he approached, "Gianni, it was a dangerous game that I played at, a fatal one for Sabine. It seemed so easy at first and the money was so grand and harmed no one, an escort type of thing and grand parties with the famous and rich of Rome. It was so easy, so much money…fine things…seemed as if it had no end. But then things got dark and a bit rough with rumors among the working girls and events with, shall I say, underworld types and drugs. Then the scandal and Sabine's suicide and now I am scared, darling."

"It wasn't a suicide," he glared at her as she dropped the cigarette and moved away from him and sat down at the dressing table to stare into the mirror. He crushed the cigarette then went to the set, and picked up the fallen Bikini top and brought it over to her. She took the top with indifference and laid it on the dresser and looked into the mirror again. Her face was lit with the stark unforgiving light of the small lights of the make-up mirror frame.

"She was murdered? Murder, Gianni!"

The lights feathered the edges of her image as her eyes looked up at him in the mirror when he stood behind her. "There are people who have me marked and maybe you, too. I'm being followed and they could be following you, because you know too much. You have to tell me all you know and then we have to figure out what we can do to save ourselves."

Jill looked away, "What are you talking about? I don't know anything! Nothing, I am in enough trouble already, Gianni. Elio sacked me because he found me using drugs and that I met with the police about Sabine. I'm not to talk to anyone about her case, the police threatened me. They are interested in the escort business she ran."

She stood up and went to the chair where her shift dress was and took a loosely formed cigarette from a pack that was on the chair under the dress, lit it with a wax match from the box on the chair, and took a long drag, then she moved toward him, "Are we working on the shoot or am I being interrogated by you as well?"

He studied her as she came to him, "There's a black Alfa out there tailing me, I hope it's the police. Whoever it is, saw you come in. You better hope it is the police as well and you better tell me everything you know about Sabine's enterprise, so I can figure out what to do."

"What can you do?"

"I have friends and a relative who can help."

She looked at him nervously, then smiled anxiously, and moved away to sit down at the dressing table again. After a long drag from the loosely formed cigarette, she turned to the mirror and exhaled smoke, as her eyes fixed on him advancing towards her in the mirror, "I have been warned to talk to no one about the case by the police. I'm here to finish the shoot only, since you are in a business mood and not in the mood for fun. So, am I to be camera ready, *maestro* darling?" An ironic smile grew as her green eyes jaded into an uneasy stare and looked at him in the mirror.

He recognized the look in her eyes and then the smell.

"That's hash you lit up, you dumb bitch!" He moved quickly to her side and grabbed at the joint.

She stood and pushed his hand aside, "Now that's the Gianni I know, the one with passion. Not the Gianni who tells stories that upset me. And we will work together today and on the beach near your place near Pompeii tomorrow and I will do anything you say, Gianni, because I am in trouble and without funds and I need the work. And no reefer will prevent me from working today."

She pushed him away, then sat at the dressing table, turned to the mirror again, and smoked the hashish and looked at herself in the mirror, and then at him in the mirror standing over her, and laughed at him, "My breasts are still firm and formed well, thankfully, no sag, even at my age. Check my boobs, darling? In Paris, there were wine buckets of ice at the cabaret stage wings to raise nipples and tins of rouge to tint them with our fingers, just as we went on. Ah! The French, no neo-realism for them, not like Romans, where there are no cosmetics when it comes to sex."

The reefer hung from the side of her mouth as she took time to silently finish her make-up and gave a few quick strokes to her hair with a brush, then she stood, and picked up the Bikini top and put it on, crushed the reefer butt in the ash tray on the dresser top, and announced, "I am camera ready, *maestro*!"

He moved away from her and went to the set to check the camera, "Was Estelle in the chorus with you in Paris?"

She came onto the set, and began to chat wistfully testing his reaction, "Estelle, dear Estelle. You with her… Thought you and I could be a number after Annabelle left you, even if I have a few short years on you. But young Estelle… She is young, quite young, you know, and she has entered the scene. Can't say I blame you. She draws crowds to the cabaret show, and now that Sabine is dead, she'll be the only headliner.

"She was huge in Paris, you know. She had an act at the tawdry cabaret where I was in the chorus. It was a cheap dump, where drunken sailors and perverts congregated at the bar to gawk at our nipples, all raised by ice and brightened with rouge. She was an instant success at sixteen, illegal, you know, even in Paris to perform nude. No one else knew her age at the cabaret, except me, because I got her the false identity papers from a mafia type who took a special interest in me. I met her in Paris at a party near the Sorbonne. She told me she had come to Paris to meet up with friends studying at university and she didn't want to go back to London.

"She claimed she studied ballet for years and tried for the Crazy Horse and Lido, but they would not touch her because she had no proof she was of age. I sort of took her under my wing as an older sister would and helped her out. She had no reservations about doing a strip and I helped her with it. It was a strip that even the showgirls appreciated. We called it the Virgin Spring, a cross between Snow White and Josephine Baker. She did an attractive high-kick that was impressive because of her long legs and danced on toes on the stage set of a forest, stripped, and entered into a projected image of a spring bringing down the house.

"She, being so fair and so obviously youthful, brought attention from the Gendarmes and the management chose to sack her, rather than risk being closed down. Elio, who visits Paris all the time shopping for showgirls, saw her last performance and contracted with her to perform at his Cabaret Rome by Nite when he found out she was sacked. Rome having a greater appreciation of precocious youthful blonds than Paris, it was easy for Elio to arrange things with the law. As you know, all is possible in Rome with the right contacts. She insisted I come with her and Elio hired me for the showgirl chorus line. He had no objections since I was blond, British and a showgirl with nice boobs, all the assets necessary for success at his cabaret"

"Was Estelle a part of Sabine's enterprise?"

"Now, I see why you asked me about her. If she were, I would have known. I specifically told Sabine not to get her involved."

"Annabelle was." He started focusing the camera on Jill.

"How did you find out?"

"Sabine told me when I used her for a shoot shortly before she died." He came from behind the camera and adjusted the lights.

"Annabelle was more involved than I was and had things going on in the dark with her as well."

She watched him return to the camera and ask, "What things, Jill?"

"I was in it for the fast one nighters, quick cash of the escort business. Annabelle used it to climb."

"What about the under-age girls?"

"How can you tell now days, I would have never taken Estelle for sixteen once she was made-up, besides, there was not much contact among the working girls, really all of it done by phone."

"But there were rooms with clandestine young immigrant girls." He studied Jill.

"I know nothing about that. And I am silent from now on about the subject as the police warned me to be."

She adjusted her Bikini top again and moved to the mark that Gianni indicated in front of the white background screen and studied him as he reluctantly turned away and went to adjust the jell on a light. When he was satisfied, he adjusted the light stand to produce a feathered light that caught her eyes in a soft glow.

Jill smiled at him as he went behind the camera, "Gianni, we can leave for Pompeii immediately after we finish the shoot here, am I not right?"

She waited while he left the camera and went to the reflector on her right, immediately off her shoulder and then asked him again, "Am I not right, darling?"

"Right about what Jill?"

"The shoot on the coast, we can leave immediately after this shoot. I have the urge for the beach and the sea and to get out of the city and away from the whole sordid mess, forget Sabine and everyone!"

He went behind the camera again, "I feel the same, but I thought I was to pick you up tomorrow and go. You didn't bring clothes and things for yourself today, I planned staying a few days and visiting relatives and friends I knew as a kid. And I have a special chore to do."

"Don't worry about a change of clothes for me. I'll fish out something from your costume rack. There are lots I can wear here and I left an overnight at your studio in Pompeii the last time," she smiled at him, though he never locked at her, as he made adjustments to the lens and positioned the tripod.

"What about something to eat before we leave?" he asked softly.

"I am not hungry... You know me. I eat less than a sparrow. We can eat later on the way. Do you think we could find that cantina in the hills outside Rome? There was that place we stopped and we ate on the *terrazzo* under the shade of a straw canopy and you ordered that special lamb plate...and the wine was so great and fresh tasting."

He smiled. "The great sauce and the hot bread. It was fall when you came with me for the shoot in the ruins, last year, was it?"

"Last year in late September and I had the quail the cook had shot that morning with pellets still lodged in them with the cool white wine."

He remembered and the smile grew for a second, then he focused the camera, and ordered, "Set now!"

The shoot lasted till mid-afternoon and it was clear to Gianni that the energy Jill showed was from the influence of the drugs but never affected her modeling. She knew how to pose for cameos and gesture profiles in the costumes and beachwear in front of the background screen and she never wasted time in setting at his commands. Then, as he reset lights and camera angles for each costume, she would run off quickly and change and respond to the camera and his directions alertly. When he decided to break the session, he made coffee while she showered. When she finished, she slipped on her brief and the shift dress, and then took a few casual things from the costumes rack, and threw them into the swimwear costumes case for the shoot on the beach. They left for Pompeii after she took a small sip of the coffee Gianni had made.

He always took the Appian route south that crossed Lazio and into the cultivated hills of the *Castelli Romani*, where they stopped for the wine at the cantina that Jill remembered. She cradled the wine glass and sipped the cool white wine that refreshed with the feel of spring water, as they sat at the *terrazzo* table, looking at the ordered vineyards that spread to the horizon and found the late day sunlight.

"Darling. It is peaceful here," she stood up and walked from the *terrazzo* and into a row of vines.

As he came to her she turned to him and kissed him. "Pity, there is Estelle. I feel a bit guilty, even about my indiscreet advances this early a.m.; lucky for her, you are an honorable scoundrel. It's a part of your charm, I think. You are a bad boy and the girls at the club would love a shagging with you, who knows how many have in the years you've been around. It only makes you more desirable with them, along with the nice cash you pay for shoots."

She fondled his hair, then her fingers, traced the scar above his right eye, “Does it hurt darling?”

She didn’t wait for a reply and kissed the scar, then his cheek and then his lips. When she felt no response, she stepped away and noticed the dark concern in his eyes, as they focused beyond her. She turned to follow their direction and saw a black car on the siding of the road near the edge of an expansive grove.

“What is it?”

“We have to leave now.”

He turned quickly and went into the cantina and paid as she came to him. He looked at her with concern and took her hand and led her to the car. They drove off as soon as she closed the door and then he shifted to high speed and burned rubber after reaching the paved road. He knew that he could try and out-pace the black Alfa and his Maserati could handle the sharp curves of a small road he had discovered years ago when he came to the hills to avoid the summer heat of Rome.

He knew that there was a cross roads five kilometers down the road. A left would take him back into the hills a right to the coast. Immediately, after the left of the divide there was a tight road on the left not completely paved, which the farmers used to access orchards in the high grounds of the hills. There were a number of tight turns and a turn off that returned to the main road.

He raced away from the Alfa, which took time to leave, because the driver was out of the car. Probably relieving himself, Gianni thought. When he reached the divide, he took the left, then seconds later, a tight left onto the farm road, raced up the hillside, and took the quick left turn that led back to the main road. As the Maserati raced down to meet the main-road, he saw in the rear-view mirror that the Alfa had missed the turn off to the returning road. When the Maserati reached the main road again, it returned to the crossroads and raced down the road that led to the coast.

In all of this, Jill was silent. She slumped into the plush leather car seat and periodically looked at him and was taken by his agility in shifting and commanding the steering wheel in the sharp turns. At times, she glared in fear out her window to see the passenger side tires test the cliff edges of the small-unpaved road. When they made the turn onto the coast road and he was able to drive at flat out high speed, she asked demurely, “Have we lost them?”

“For now!” Gianni replied somberly.

They stopped outside Formia; where the road met the coast and hid the car behind a small open *taverna* and had an early dinner of pasta and mixed catch seafood and a liter of local white wine under a straw roof pergola of the *terrazzo* that opened to the beach. Jill finished a glass quickly and he poured a second for her and saw the nervousness in her eyes as she glared at him and asked, “What does all this mean, Gianni?”

“I think we are in something we don’t know how to get out of.”

He drank the wine deliberately and looked out to sea.

Her eyes fixed him, “We?”

“Yes, unfortunately, because you’re with me,” he replied.

She looked at him for a moment, then stood and made her way from the *terrazzo* to the beach and the water’s edge. The sun broke the haze, as it sought the horizon and lifted petals of light on the gentle swells of the Mediterranean. The light of the failing sun lit the soft translucent summer fabric of her lace shift and revealed her appealing showgirl form that caught the eye of a fisherman mending his net on the beach near her.

When she returned, she sat quietly, and began to eat, but took just two forks full of pasta, then refreshed her glass of wine and looked at the setting sun as she drank. "I didn't count on this…"

Gianni suddenly grabbed her wrist before she finished her thought and whispered in her ear as he looked at the two men at the table off to the right and the suspicious glance of the man facing him, "Smile now, darling, and kiss me as if you needed a shag."

She hesitated a moment, then placed a hand around his neck, and kissed him passionately, then, suddenly, he upset her glass pouring wine onto her shift. She jumped knocking over her chair and he came to his feet apologizing, "Sorry, darling!"

Then he laughed, as did the suspicious couple to his right, and immediately led a confused Jill from the *terrazzo*. He paid the bill and led her quickly to the car and drove off.

As they sped along the coast, he looked nervously in the rear-view mirror, and apologized again to Jill. "Sorry, I had to do that to test the reaction of a suspicious looking couple. Especially, the guy who was looking at your bum very scandalously visible in the sunlight through the light shift you have on, darling."

She busied herself blotting the wine stain, "My bum, as you indelicately put it, has been notoriously useful and helped my success in my showgirl career."

"Exactly right, notorious ass, and more, darling!" he called out and accelerated the car on the straightaway that ran along the beach near Formia.

It was dark when the Maserati pulled off the small road and into a driveway and stopped at the side of a two-story stone building. When they entered the studio from the second-floor *terrazzo*, he turned on the light and was stunned at the disorder. The file draws were all cleaned out with their contents scattered on the floor, the clothes racks emptied of costumes and piled in disorder in center of the studio, the costumes in some cases torn and thrown about, the divan cushions cut open, and the kitchen cabinets emptied with contents thrown in the sink and on the kitchen table. The bathroom cabinet was emptied and some vials of painkillers and medicines thrown on the floor. The mattress in the bedroom was off the bed frame and ripped in a number of places.

He ran to the *armadio,* which was left open with his clothes thrown on the floor and found the wristwatch his father had given him and put it in his pocket. As he left the bedroom, he saw Jill standing in the studio space at the background screen that had been overturned and went to her and commanded, "Come on, we have to leave now!"

She quickly followed him out the door and down the stairs and went into the car. He ran back up the stairs and grabbed the open make-up case from the floor and put it back in order and took it, then he grabbed the tri-pod that lay next to it and went to the door, turned off the light switch and went out the door, which locked easily, even though it had been forced.

When he reached the bottom of the stairs, he found a lean unshaven figure waiting for him, "Gianni, you are back again. You left this morning so early with the blond. Is she all right, I see her in the car now with you? I was afraid this morning with all the noise and the way she rushed out and you after her, I thought you had a lover's spat. A loud one, I must admit, that disturbed Teresa, you know how my wife is about the girls you bring here."

"Sorry, Nando," he replied nervously, "Just a bit of fun, you understand, too much wine last night. Tell Teresa I am deeply sorry." He smiled and tapped Nando's shoulder as a gesture of friendship and turned and went to his car quickly.

Nando followed him; "You have the Maserati now and a different car this morning."

Gianni turned quickly to his downstairs neighbor, "What car this morning?"

"The black one."

"The Alfa?"

"I don't know but it was black."

Nando's eyes followed Gianni as he placed the make-up case and tripod in the trunk containing his cameras and two large self-standing reflectors and small spot, closed the trunk quickly, and then went to the driver's side door, opened it and sat behind the wheel, and closed the door with a slam. He smiled at Nando, who called out when the car began to move, "A large black car!" Then Nando waived to Jill and gave a smile as they drove off.

Jill waved back and gave a timid courteous smile as the car drove off. Gianni quick dialed a number on his car phone and then spoke in a controlled tone of voice, "Ciao yes, it's Gianni, I thought that I could stay at your place this evening… Yes… No, I have an English model with me. My studio has no electricity right now and therefore, also no hot water for a shower and I thought we could stay the night…yes…then Paola is there and you will call her…as always."

"And that was about?" Jill asked.

"A place to stay and we can finish the photo-shoot and I won't miss the deadline in Paris and, my dear, if I work it the right way, you will be safe and I can find out who were the people who broke into my studio earlier today and perhaps start putting together the scattered pieces to the puzzle."

"And where is this place we are going to?" Jill studied him closely.

"At the edge of the sea. A villa meant for Caesar and owned by one of the most powerful men in these parts. My dear, Uncle Armando, Don Armando, for respect to everyone who is not family."

The Maserati flew along the straight away that skirted under the steep cliffs of Mount Faito and then into the tunnel that cut through the mountain to come out onto the edge of cliffs that overlooked the Bay of Naples. He chose the old road rather than the new highway to go through the small villages that, at one time, were inhabited only by fishermen and their families, but now had become bedroom communities with new construction condominiums, a number, of which, were built by the construction company his uncle Armando owned.

The white convertible made a sharp left turn at a crossroads on to the road leading to Sant' Agata and the Amalfi drive that twisted along the shadows of the imposing mountains and skirted the edge of cliffs that dropped off into the shores of the Mediterranean. He drove along the challenging Amalfi drive at a speed that alarmed Jill, who glared at the sharp curves and measured the car's drift to the edge of the cliffs, then let out a plea for caution that brought an incorrigible smile from Gianni, but then he lamented as she touched his arm and whispered nervously, "Let's just get where we are going without the grand prix experience, darling."

When the car reached the turn off to Positano, it slipped cautiously into a sharp curve, then made a right turn that led to the gates of a large villa, where Gianni sounded the horn and got out, looked up at the villa terrace, and waited until a young woman appeared on the *terrazzo* and waved at him, then disappeared.

When he got back into the car, the gates opened and the car made its way to a parking area at the side of a walkway that led up a path to a garden with a swimming pool. When they left the car, they walked up the pathway and were met by the young woman seen on the terrace. She was tall with long brown hair that covered her shoulders and wore dark framed eyeglasses. She immediately embraced Gianni and kissed him on both cheeks, and then she stepped away and looked at Jill with a sober formal glance.

"Jill, *piacere,*" the showgirl said warmly and extended a hand to the young woman.

"I speak English, I am Paola," she said coldly and shook Jill's hand, then turned to Gianni, "I arranged everything myself, you will have the large bedroom that faces the sea and the model has the guest cabana by the pool. It has a shower and she will be fine there all alone, no one to bother

her. Come. I have prepared something to eat and brought a bottle of the *Toscana* from the cantina you like so much, as well as some white that the model may prefer. *Zi'* Armando will be here tomorrow afternoon, he told me that when he called. So, we will have the place to ourselves tonight and most of tomorrow. He told me that you had a problem at your studio at Pompeii."

Gianni smiled at her and took her by the arm and explained as they walked to the villa, "The electricity was out and no hot water and I have to complete a shoot for Paris and thought we could do everything in the garden and at poolside, instead of my studio and the deserted beach near Pompeii."

Paola shrugged, "You know about those things. I set up something to eat on the *terrazzo* for tonight."

They followed her into a large living room with bay windows overlooking the town and the sea, and then Paola led them out the sliding door and onto a *terrazzo*, where a round table was prepared with a family size bowl of Mediterranean salad and a variety of cheese and prosciutto, bread and breadsticks and three place settings with lit candles.

"I thought something light like this is what you always preferred, Gianni, in the evening." She touched his shoulder, moving him to a seat, then turned to Jill, and said coldly, "I hope this will be to your liking."

"Yes," Jill smiled and sat down and returned the cold stare from Paola, "And you are so thoughtful, my dear, at your age."

"Paola is my cousin and is at a local institute—" Gianni interrupted.

Paola glared at him and said sternly, "I graduated and I am at the University of Salerno and we are not cousins, as I have said many times. We share Uncle Armando but we are not cousins."

Paola sat down quickly and poured wine for him and then her glass and drank as she watched the two guests fill their plates with the food she had laid out.

"Are you not eating?" Jill asked, as she leaned past Paola and took the bottle of red wine and filled her glass as well, took some prosciutto, wrapped into a long slice of bread, then took an irritated bite, and glared back at the young figure, whose eyeglasses reflected the light from the candle in front of her dish, giving the impression that the university student was glaring at the English showgirl, as if she were a strange specimen in a science experiment.

Paola stood up without a reply and turned to the prosciutto abruptly, wrapped a slice in a piece of bread the way Jill had, and took an imitating bite of it, sat down again and took a drink of her wine, then smiled at Gianni, "The prosciutto is quite good, no?"

"Everything is quite good. You are getting to be quite the young girl and homemaker, as well as hostess," he smiled at her.

"I am at University of Salerno to study business and intend to help Zi' Armando with his enterprises and be more than just a homemaker and *caro* Gianni, I am no longer a young girl—"

Jill interrupted, "Yes she is more than a young girl, Gianni, and she has ambitions…don't you see that? Just like a man not to see things about a young woman, Paola, but you will learn to handle men, I am quite sure." Jill rolled the last word into her glass and took a drink of the red wine and then turned to her coldly, "In time."

Gianni came to his feet and broke Paola's sullen silence, "Shall we all have a nice look at the view." He took Jill by the arm, almost upsetting the wine glass she was holding, brought her to her feet, and led her to the *terrazzo* railing. He whispered in her ear before Paola could join them, "Cut it out, darling."

"You know best," Jill smiled, while mimicking Paola's use of *'caro* Gianni' and enjoyed her wine, as they stood on the *terrazzo*, looking at the village below, asleep in the shadows, slipping onto the single lane road that wound down through the cluster of buildings to the beach.

"It is quiet at this hour," Paola's soft voice at his side caused Gianni to turn to her, as she fit her arm under his and drew her body closely to him.

"Quiet indeed and I have the need of a rest after that adventurous trip, darlings," Jill turned away from them and went to the table, set the wine glass, and called back to them, "I can find the guest cabin and I'll get my things from the car, as little of them as there are, darling!"

"I can show you everything in the cabana." Paola said, helpfully, as Jill began to leave.

"No need," was the reply and Jill left them.

Gianni held Paola's arm when she tried to follow Jill and admonished her in Italian, "You were naughty to Jill. You have grown since last I saw you but a mature woman knows how to be polite, even if displeased."

"I need no lectures on etiquette from you! Especially about a woman like her," came a caustic Italian reply, then the angry young woman turned from him abruptly and went to the sliding door and disappeared.

After finishing his glass of wine, he went down to the car, and took the costumes case from the trunk and the large Leica camera and went up to the cabana, knocked, and waited till Jill opened and let him in. He placed the costumes case on the floor by the bed and the camera on a nearby chair, as she started to slip off her shift dress to take a shower, and he left to take out the camera tripod from the car trunk. When he returned with them to the cabana, Jill was adjusting the water of the shower, wearing a bath towel. She turned quickly when he came in and the towel began to fall. She was readjusting it just as there was a knock at the door. She stepped behind Gianni, as he turned to go the door but she grabbed his arm and whispered to him, "It must be Paola… The shower."

He turned, looked at her concern, and stepped quickly into the shower after turning off the water. She pulled the shower curtain to hide him, then went to the door, and opened it enough to poke her head out to find Paola holding soap and extra towels.

The young figure pushed the door open and stepped in quickly, scanned the room, and announced, "I have towels and soap. I went to Gianni's room to bring him towels but he was not there. Do you know where he went?"

"No, darling, he left these things here for tomorrow's shoot and went off." Jill took the soap and towels from Paola, "Thanks. I saw there was none; now if you please I'd like to take a shower and am not dressed to entertain."

"Check to see if the water is hot enough. I have turned on the water heater shortly before you both arrived," Paola insisted and folded her arms.

Jill turned to cover the shower curtain with her body, leaned into the shower, and turned on the cold-water tap.

"Did you turn on the hot one?" Paola demanded.

Jill turned on the hot one.

"You have to wait for it to get hot," Paola insisted.

Jill waited for a few seconds with her hand under the water and then turned to Paola with a patronizing smile, "It is hot enough now, darling."

"Of that, I am not sure!" A smug smile came to the university student's lips as she adjusted her glasses, then turned, and left the cabana.

Gianni jumped from the shower completely soaked and upset as Jill laughed, "Poor Gianni, you'll be shagging showgirls in Rome with all the liberty you want, only to end up entrapped by your young, impetuous, and calculating cousin from the University of Salerno."

A Villa for Caesar

The next morning Gianni woke in the guest bedroom overlooking the sea and saw that his wet clothes had been taken from the balcony, where he left them the night before. He had a change in the overnight he brought from Rome, showered, and dressed. When he went to the patio by the pool, he saw Jill and Paola having breakfast. He asked about his wet clothes and Paola said she had picked them up earlier that morning as well as Jill's things and given them to Marina, the daytime housekeeper, to take care of. Then Paola invited him to take breakfast and then left for Salerno on her Vespa scooter for a course in finance.

"Paola knows what she wants and it is you darling," Jill remarked as they sat together.

"Don't be silly. She's just a bit more impetuous than other kids her age and quite bright."

"Too bright," Jill poured coffee for him and smiled ironically, which he caught with a shrug.

After they finished breakfast, Gianni set up the tripod and camera at the poolside that overlooked the town, then went to the car, and took a freestanding reflector and small spotlight on a stand and set them up at the side of the pool for the shoot and used the panorama of the town stretching along surrounding hills as background. Jill changed into a single piece costume Gianni wanted because the sun was not bright and hot enough at the time for Bikinis. They worked with six pieces, each having different cut away backs that allowed for Jill's long blond hair, at times, wet and giving off a sheen from pool water to compose on her bare back.

Before the housekeeper left at one, she laid out their dried and ironed clothes on deck chairs and set up a late lunch of summer salad and fruit with *calamari* seared in oil and seasoned with basil and the bottle of the sweet local white from the night before on ice. When they stopped to eat, Paola returned and joined them. She seemed at ease with them, even cracking a joke about *Zi'* Armando's inability to be on time, even when he had promised her earlier that morning by phone to be there for the lunch she had asked the housekeeper to prepare. But, then, she said he texted that he would be late. When they finished lunch, she refused help clearing the dirty dishes and insisted the guests finish their work.

The shoot continued under the high Mediterranean sun of the afternoon that produced the warm intense light conducive to the tropical nude look of the string Bikinis. They worked rapidly with a dozen poses for each costume in different angles and different light. Jill indiscreetly changed behind the reflector screen and at times, capriciously dove nude in the water for an effect, as the camera took motion action stills of her, and then she would pose in a wet look or dry herself and change costumes at poolside behind the screen as Gianni reset the camera. Neither of them had noticed that Paola had come to the far side of the pool dressed in her own black Bikini and stretched out on a recliner.

When the sunlight dissipated because of rising clouds, Gianni decided to stop and Jill cheered and ran topless, waiving her arms in relief and dove into the pool. When she surfaced, she saw Paola peering at her in sunglasses and swam off quickly to the ladder away from her, got out of the pool, picked up a towel, and ran into the cabana. Gianni looked up at his model passing him as he released the camera from the tripod and then saw Paola on the other side of the pool, who was focused on the scene.

He took the camera, came over to her, and sat on the beach chair next to her and smiled timidly, "Jill's a bit free, she's a topless showgirl in a cabaret in Rome; she thinks nothing of being nude with an audience."

Paola turned to him. "She shows that."

"It's all professional for me, you see. And good for the camera lens when a model is a bit uninhibited and knows how to use her body." He held the camera out to her, "Look! You can see how natural she is with the string Bikinis. It's because she's used to showing off nude. She's perfect for this kind of shoot."

Paolo took off her sunglasses and smiled disingenuously, reached back, and undid her Bikini top, sat up, as it fell to the ground, and stood in a pose in front of him, "Does your camera lens like this?" She smirked at him then ran to the diving board and went out to the edge, extended her arms for a dive, and froze at the sound of her uncle's angry voice.

"Paola! *Sei pazza!*"

Then she dove into the water and swam to the far end of the pool, got out, and ran off under the barrage of his angry invectives.

"Are you mad exposing yourself? What do you think you are; a French tart that contaminates our beaches every summer?" He turned sharply to Gianni as he advanced up the path, "You are responsible!"

"I am not!" came the protest.

"Then how do you explain this? You with the camera, she's posing for you nude!"

"Paola did not! I did!" Jill's voice caused Don Armando to turn quickly. Then, suddenly, he stepped back and became quiet. As he studied her advance toward him, his eyes became more and more somber at the sight of Jill in a white pool towel advancing.

Jill studied him, then stopped her advance abruptly, and looked nervously at Gianni, who stood up quickly and went to his uncle's side, "Jill is the English model I told you I had to bring for the swimwear shoot for Paris. I only photographed her, you can see in the camera. Every image is of her modeling."

He extended the camera to his uncle, who ignored it as his eyes focused on Jill, who resumed her advance more deliberately.

"Gianni is right. I saw it myself. Paola took off her top and went for a dive without Gianni even noticing, because he was checking out the shoot of me in the camera." Jill smiled softly and extended a hand cautiously, when she reached the two men, "You are, I take it, Don Armando and I am Jill…Gianni's model."

"Yes, I see," Don Armando loosened his tie nervously with his left hand, as he shook her hand with his right, then took a few uncertain steps from her, and took off his summer gray linen jacket, "Let's go inside and get something cool to drink."

Jill smiled again, "I'll shower and dress in the cabana. I think the two of you have plenty to talk about alone." She took the camera Gianni offered to her and moved away toward the cabana quickly.

Don Armando led his nephew up the path and into the large living room and then went to the bar, poured them both a cognac with ice and asked him coldly, "How do you know that model… What was her name?"

"Jill, she works as a showgirl in Rome and model, I have used her a number of times," Gianni's words were studied as he noticed an unusual disquiet in his usually jovial uncle, who moved away from the bar and gave him a glass, and took a drink from his glass. Then a bell sounded and he went to the large bay window that faced the garden and the pool as well as the entrance to the villa, where a black Alfa had pulled up to the closed front gate and the driver stood at the gate's bell.

Don Armando looked back at his nephew, who had stirred at the sound of the bell, then went to a button on the wall near the glass door, and pushed it to open the front gate. Gianni came to the window and watched as the Alfa drove into the parking area and stopped between his Maserati and his uncle's black Mercedes. Then he turned to Don Armando, who looked at him coldly.

"We have visitors interested in the events you got so stupidly involved in Rome." His uncle went to the sliding door and opened it.

When his nephew turned back to the window, he saw two men in dark suits advance deliberately up the garden walk just as Paola, in jeans and a white summer blouse, ran past them, and got on her Vespa scooter and rode off quickly out the open gate. When the men arrived at the sliding glass door, Don Armando greeted them. The taller man remained outside. The shorter man came in. He wore large black-rimmed glasses and had a slight mustache and was bald, except for the gray at his temples.

Don Armando led the man to the bar and quickly went behind, put his drink down, and took two brandy glasses, dropped a single ice cube in each, and poured cognac into both glasses and handed one to the visitor, and then pointed to the other glass, "For your man outside?"

"Better no." The visitor put his glass on the bar top and looked at Gianni, then back at his host and spoke formally, "Don Armando, I called the commissioner to have this meeting with you, sir, before the delicate situation in Rome could get more complicated, and he has designated me the inspector in charge of the investigation at this time."

"I understand Marco," the host shrugged, took his own drink, and went over to the large, white leather couch at the other end of the room, motioned to the inspector to come over, and sit and then turned to Gianni and pointed to the white, leather chair on his left and waited for both men to sit, then he asked after sitting near his guest, "Now, what do you have to say about this mess in Rome, inspector?"

The inspector folded his hands as if in prayer, then looked boldly at his host, "Don Armando, we, in Rome, understand the concerns you have for your nephew and his safety and believe me, I am giving my full attention to the case, realizing the sensitive nature of what he is dealing with and that is why the commissioner agreed to this meeting. My department, as you know, deals only with sensitive investigations of government matters."

The detective unfolded his hands and pulled out a small pad from his jacket pocket, opened it quickly, and flipped some pages until he stopped and studied one, then looked up at his host, "What is disquieting at this point and more immediately, Don Armando, is that your nephew left Rome with a certain showgirl, known to the Rome police as 'Snow White' because of her affection for cocaine and please, excuse me, for bringing this up, her name in art is 'Jill Hump-free' as a performer at the 'Cabaret Rome by Nite.' She also worked at the escort service that we are all concerned about involving the scandal that has been publicized in the media."

Gianni leaned forward insisting, "I had nothing to do with Sabine's bordello and I did not know that any of the showgirls at the Cabaret were involved. I used them as models. That's all."

The inspector interrupted him, "Many of the showgirls have been questioned and are still being investigated. But your association with them and with Sabine is a matter of record and presents an element of suspicion to the investigators in Rome. The average young man does not have a relationship with a showgirl who operated a criminal enterprise and was found dead under suspicious circumstances and also has an intimate relationship with a number of showgirls who happen to be involved in the same criminal enterprise! I hope, Don Armando, you realize the position of the investigators." The inspector looked at both men, and settled back in his seat.

Armando took a long drink from his glass, then stood, and went to the bar and refreshed it with more cognac, turned to the inspector, and frowned, "I realize the information about my nephew's associations is a red flag for the magistrate in Rome. But the fact is that everything you have said about my nephew shows that his only crime is his professional relationship with showgirls in the course of his business, and he may have had an amorous relationship with one or more of them. And that is the evidence against him. But you must understand that he is my nephew and that relationship has a political charge to it that could explode into a media scandal about me, Marco!"

The inspector moved uneasily in his seat, "Certainly, and that is why I am involved with this case. That is why, I am here to clarify things and insure that the investigation does not become a political witch-hunt dragging in your nephew. I hope you can appreciate my candor here and my willingness to settle things with regards to justice in his case and not have it tried in the media."

Armando moved from the bar and towards the inspector, "I appreciate the commissioner putting you on the case, I have always heard good things about you and that your special investigation office has always handled sensitive cases like this effectively."

The inspector stood, "Rest assured, Don Armando, we will proceed with utmost caution in this delicate matter, I can assure you of that. But I must bring up a matter that involves your nephew. It has to do with what happened in New York or more precisely, Brooklyn about five years ago."

"That's history and settled," Gianni interrupted and stood up.

The investigator flashed a concerned glance at him, "The matter of your association with some undesirables in Brooklyn and to a stripper who overdosed in your Brooklyn loft and later died is a tangential matter, since the case has been closed with no charges against you. I put it to rest as disturbing as it is similar to the death of Sabine, who was a showgirl and involved in the underworld sex market, as was the stripper in Brooklyn.

"But there is something else, something more alarming. We have information that certain underworld characters in Rome, who have connections with Brooklyn, don't have your well-being in mind, Gianni. They probably know you are being guarded by my men and have not attempted anything so far. But what aggravates the people I put on to protect your safety is that you try and shake them or play silly games on dangerous roads as you did yesterday in the hills outside Rome. You are simply irritating my men and making their job more difficult and endangering your life."

Gianni became angry, "You are making my life hell. I'm sure you wired Elio in the cabaret when I met him and Estelle at her place was probably wired as well. You are trying to entrap me!"

The inspector's voice ripped back, "That is not the case!"

Don Armando quickly interrupted, “I am sure, Marco, that you are acting honorably in this. I have confidence in this and will say so to your superiors in Rome.” He put his arm around the inspector and walked him to the sliding glass door, and he watched the inspector go down to the black Alfa with the driver, then he closed the sliding door, and stood with Gianni and watched the black sedan turn and drive past the open gate and then it disappeared up the road that led them out of Positano.

“Is your model the one they are talking about?” Armando asked, as he took his nephew by the arm.

“Yes. But I did not know about her involvement with the escort operation until yesterday.”

“I see. And the people in Rome who have connections in Brooklyn?”

“I don’t know. It could be someone in Rome making it up.”

“Who then?” His uncle looked at his nephew with concern.

“I am not sure. But I will find out.”

“Be careful, don’t do anything dangerous and contact me if you have information. I can protect you, my boy. Just contact me.”

His uncle placed a hand on his nephew’s shoulder, “Find Paola. Perhaps, we could have something to eat together?”

“She ran off and took her scooter.”

“Why?”

“A bit of embarrassment, I think.”

His uncle shrugged, “Over my reaction, I imagine. She has a great respect for me. Too much, I think. But it was a shock to see her like that. She is still a child to me. Listen, she's probably home, you know the place down by the great garage at the beach."

"Of course, I know it."

"Then go to her and see if she will come back here."

Gianni shrugged, "She won't because of Jill."

"What happened?"

"A bit of cat fighting between them."

Don Armando put an arm around his nephew, "Go to her anyway and bring her flowers from me and tell her that I am not upset. Then take her in your sports car and let her drive it. She tells me how much she loves your car."

"Fine, then," his nephew smiled.

His uncle watched his nephew leave and go down the garden path to the cabana and knock at the door. When it opened, Jill stood in the doorway, listened to him for a few seconds, gave him a kiss, and returned into the cabana, closing the door behind her. When Gianni reached his car, he drove out and his uncle pressed the remote button to close the villa gate behind it. Then he took his drink and went onto the *terrazzo* to finish the glass of cognac and look out over the town.

Centuries ago, Positano had been a refuge for pirates and a place of danger for travelers on schooners attacked by the pirates in longboats, hiding in the coves along the coast. The village was a smugglers' haven, as well and a natural redoubt for rebels and pirates to defend against the military forces of the Spanish King of Naples.

But now, Armando looked out over a place for the affluent and tourists that no longer belonged to that story. A place he grew up in and loved and fought for when the

American Rangers landed and scaled the cliffs from the sea and battled the German panzers that blocked the Amalfi road and the two Eighty Eights at Sant' Agata. At fifteen, he was fighting Germans and ran from behind the enemy lines to the Americans, bringing them information about the enemy; and led them along the hidden mountain run-off to avoid the German tanks on the road, and then up the slopes of Monte Faito on the path that only goat herders knew, and across the fields and the farms to come up behind the German Eighty Eight guns that threatened the landing at Salerno, so that the Rangers could take out the German crews with the fifty caliber machine guns and a recoilless rocket launcher they had brought.

He remembered the blistered bodies of the Germans who he had seen kill his people and he had learned to hate and when the Americans liberated the town, he was given a medal and hailed by the entire town as a hero. Now that moment of honor was fading away and a sense of shame overtook him; overshadowing the work he had done and the empire he had created since that time of his youth.

He finished the cognac and turned to find Jill at the entrance to the *terrazzo*, wearing a revealing beachwear covering from the swimwear shoot. "Shall I still call you, Renato?" she smiled softly and came to him as he opened his arms.

The Maserati made its way deliberately down the road that led to the main beach, as it negotiated past the crowds coming up from the beach that mingled with the tourist strollers and shoppers. The car came to a stop in front of an open vendor selling flowers and Gianni reached from the car and pointed out a bunch, paid for it, and drove down to the weathered front of the building facing a garage at the entrance of the old Saracen quarter and stopped. Then he began honking the horn under Paola's balcony. When he saw no one came out to look down at the noise, he called out her name. When there still was no reply, he sat on the backrest of the driver's seat, placed a foot on the horn, and repeatedly called out Paola between the horn blares.

Suddenly, a head appeared from the balcony then an arm shaking a fist and then a cry to stop. But he continued, even after a small and amused crowd had gathered, until the large *portone* door opened, and Paola ran out from the *palazzo* waving her arms, "Stop this now!"

As she came to the car, he threw the bunch of flowers into her arms, and she caught them and the small crowd applauded as she jumped into the car and it drove off, once he got behind the wheel.

"The flowers by the way are complements of *Zi'* Armando, who realizes he may have over reacted to your scandalous appearance at the pool and the flowers come with his apology," he turned to her and smiled.

"Not from you then?"

"I have nothing to apologies for."

"Yes, you do."

"Yes? For what?"

"For being you," she smiled at him and asked softly, "Will you stay this time for a time or run off quickly again to Rome?"

"Would you care if I stayed?" he replied indifferently as he drove the car cautiously passed the crowded small *piazza*, leading to the old quarter where no vehicles could go.

"Don't tease me as you have always done," she replied in a firm voice.

"Probably tomorrow," he concentrated on the narrow road crowded with tourists.

"Why so soon?"

"I have to make a living; there is the rent to be paid in Rome and Pompeii and expenses at the end of the month. This car, for instance, drains money like a sink drains water and then I have to finish the studio stuff I did with Jill, edit what we did today and what I shot in Rome, and maybe shoot some more and then send it on to Paris before the first of next month. So, I have no time to play here in your tourists' paradise of Positano."

She turned to him and smiled again, "However, now, you do have time with me to make-up for your rudeness today. We will go to '*Tre Sorelle*' on the beach for an early dinner; you can park the car at the garage on that next curve. We can walk down through the old quarter and you will buy me that beautifully colored hand-dyed beach tunic I saw the other day at the shop, just before the grand steps, then we will go to dinner, and after go to Salerno and the new 'Nite' that opened just before the season."

"Why do I have to buy you anything?" he protested.

"Because you have been mean to me since you arrived with that blond. And you made me cry," she leaned over impetuously and kissed him quickly on the lips, then turned to look out the windshield, and ordered him to stop on the right at the garage entrance.

"That isn't the way you kiss a cousin!" he insisted, as he pulled the car to the entrance of the garage.

"We are not cousins!" she protested as the car stopped. She got out cradling the bunch of flowers against her breasts, waited for him until he returned from consigning the car keys to the young garage attendant. Then she led him to the small *piazza* they passed in the car and into the old quarter of the resort town.

He followed as she quickly stepped between the mingling crowd of tourists and the young, local girls arm-in-arm in Bikinis, window shopping after a day on the beach, and then down the narrow *vicolo* that was as tight as the passageways he remembered in the Kasbah in Tunis, when he went there for a shoot at Carthage with Sabine for a French fashion ad two years before. Paola finally stopped at a small shop with a front window full of beach clothes and went in and went to a rack at the end of the store to pull out a light silk semi-transparent beachwear tunic, put it on her shoulder, and then went into the dressing area.

He waited uncomfortably by the front window and had a smoke while he watched the columns of people flooding the narrow passageway, as they struggled to pass each other on the way down to the beach or on the way up from it. He remembered the same narrow passageway in winter disserted and the same shops, now open and spilling merchandise from the open show windows, boarded up after the season, then he heard Paola call him, and as he turned, he saw her approaching wearing the brightly ornamented see-through beach tunic, exposing her bare breasts under translucent colorful flower patterns. She smiled impishly "*Bella, no*?"

"Get something else or put on your bra."

"I have none and I want this to wear to the new 'Nite' you are taking me to in Salerno."

"Not with that…that way!"

"Then I'll get a Bikini, they are all on sale and put it under it and wear them both."

She went quickly to the Bikini rack and with the help of a young salesgirl found one she liked, and then went behind the curtain to change. Gianni returned the salesgirl's look with a commiserating raised eyebrow and a frustrating drag from his cigarette.

Paola appeared again in a black leather string Bikini, "You should like it, it's like the one Jill had on today by the pool but my size."

She turned and posed exaggerating her bum with only a black, leather string separating the cheeks and smiled back at him, "Remember her pose? Is it as good as this?"

She laughed, then moved to the young blushing salesgirl, who looked at him again with embarrassment, and then watched as Paola took the beach wrap from behind the dressing curtain, and put it on to pose in front of him, "Good, no! I do have taste, you think?"

She turned to see herself in the mirror, then took off her glasses, and turned to him again, "As good as any model you could have, darling!" She dragged the last word into a faint English accent, then came to him and kissed him on the lips, and before he could recover, she called to the salesgirl. "I'll wear them both and darling will pay." She smiled with a British intonation again on the word "darling" to mimic Jill's speech again.

"Only if you put your jeans on as well," Gianni glared at her and folded his arms.

"Such a prude. Go and pay, they know me and you'll get a discount." Paola put her glasses on again and laughed and went back behind the curtain and soon came out wearing her jeans and bikini top under her new beach-wrap. She handed her blouse and the string Bikini brief to the young sales-girl, who placed them and the flowers in the shop's bag and gave Gianni small change back from the hundred he gave her.

Le Tre Sorelle restaurant spanned out from the corner of the Saracen steps that opened to the beach with tables reaching the edge of the sand. A waiter was a cousin of Paola and got a table for them facing the beach and brought a wine bucket of water for her flowers. She ordered for both of them, insisting that the clams are always fresh at the restaurant and, "You can't find any better anywhere," then she ordered a bottle of white, "It is a wonderful white and quite reasonable here, darling." She pronounced the last word mimicking Jill again, which brought a smile to his face.

He found out that Paola was right about the wine; it was a bottle of Capri Bianco DOC reserve and bright and refreshing. She appeared to him to be more mature than he had ever seen her as they drank the wine. She was always assertive and at times, meddling and head strong, but tonight, he allowed her to "organize things" and instead of being irritated by her controlling manner, he was amused.

She looked at him after she tasted the wine and complained "You are quiet tonight, less combative with me and not argumentative, not like your usual contesting self. I am not sure I like a timid Gianni."

She drank again from the wine glass then took off her glasses and looked into his eyes. He finished his glass and she immediately took the bottle of wine from the bucket it shared with the flowers and filled his glass again, "There are problems, am I not right? Your eyes tell me this, don't hedge or distract me, I know you. We grew up together, you know."

"You grew up when I was already grown up."

"Don't treat me like a child."

"Tonight, I realize you are not anymore," he surrendered a smile

"I am a woman."

"A young woman, I think is the term." He drank again.

"Stop that! Stop thinking like that. I can help you. I want to help you!" She took his hand and held it tightly, "When I left the villa today, I passed two men, they were police because I saw their car, it was an inspector's car and it had Rome plates."

"They came to see Don Armando," he protested softly.

She held his hand tightly, "When he called about you last night, he was in Rome and he said to make sure I keep you at the villa. If he was in Rome, why didn't the police meet with him there?"

Gianni pulled his hand away and looked out to the beach and the sea growing dark as the sunlight weakened. Then he turned to her again, reached into his denim shirt pocket, and pulled out a packet of Marlboro cigarettes along with a box of wax matches, took out a cigarette, and avoiding her eyes, lit it. He took a long drag and looked at the sea again, "Our uncle is helping me resolve a major problem in Rome."

"It's about one of those slutty models you work with, I am sure," she said with satisfaction and took a cigarette from his packet and a match and quickly lit it, then folded her arms in contentment after leaving the cigarette to dangle from the side of her month.

He grabbed the cigarette from her mouth and threw it out onto the beach. "It makes you look cheap! Cigarettes always make women look cheap! Like drinking from a bottle."

"I am not cheap!" she sat back and frowned.

"Then don't try and act like someone that you were never raised to be." He threw his cigarette on the floor and crushed it.

"And how was I raised to be?" Paola demanded.

He studied her for a moment, "Like your aunt, Don Armando's wife. You are the image of her when she was young; he always said that about you. That's why he paid for your private school and treats you as he does. That's why he reacted as he did when he saw you topless on the pool diving board. They have no kids. That's why he always treats you as a daughter and me as a son!"

Don Armando filled Jill's glass again with wine, as they sat at the table on the terrace. She ate very little of the bread and the cheese that he found in the kitchen refrigerator, but enjoyed the red that he had bottled and shipped to him from a small vineyard near Florence.

"It is beautiful here, I can see how you wished to protect this life style." She smiled at him.

"I grew up here, my family was poor. Six of us lived in a small converted storage space at the edge of the beach with nothing. The war came when I was twelve. Back then, this town was a small fishing village built around a beach and the old smuggler and pirate hideouts. Now, look at it. I had helped the American troops when they invaded; I was just fifteen and received a medal and base privileges in Salerno and a job after the war when I was old enough. I raised some money and bought an Army excess truck from the base and then got a base contract transporting for them to U.S. bases in Italy. One truck, then three, then a fleet of excess American trucks and I had a national business with a prime client, the U.S. Military, by the time I was twenty-four.

"That simple and that fortunate and with my American military contacts, I partnered with American companies backed with Marshall Plan dollars wanting to do business in Italy in the late forties and the fifties and the corruption it brought. Then the miracle of the sixties and my company partnered with a contracting company in Naples, my wife's family owned it. We became an empire, expanding throughout Europe in the boom years of the post war. It was that simple but took its toll with all the hours on the road, the hours creating a business and the sacrifices, along with the time away from home, away from my wife. She had three miscarriages; I was away working for each of them. The last one survived for two days but died. Back then, premature births had little chance. She named him Armando and I arrived at the hospital just before he died. He was the only child we had."

"You love your wife," Jill leaned across the small table and touched his arm, then stood, and went to the railing at the edge of the *terrazzo* and looked out into the night. A full moon lit the emptiness and created shadows between the street lamps that circled down along the hillside from the coastal road to the beach, and disappeared into the bright lights of the old center with the cluster of shops illuminating the narrow Moorish passageways to the beach.

He came to her side and put his arm around her waist. "Scandal will kill her! If she finds out about us, even if it was years ago!"

"You never mentioned her in the time we were seeing each other."

"I never forgot you," he kissed her neck and then kissed her lips, and crushed her against him, "I have never stopped thinking of you. I had to stop seeing you. My wife started noticing things, picking up clues and asking questions, looking at my accounts, even asking my bookkeeper about certain expenses. I have many weaknesses. I have never been a perfect husband, as you know. Perhaps, I love too much and know God too little, but I still love you."

"And other women," Jill smiled, fondled his graying hair with her hand, and kissed his cheek, "Many other women?"

"I have weaknesses, infidelities against my wife, against you and now, this thing in Rome." He attempted to kiss her on the lips again but she moved away.

"The thing with Gianni and Sabine?" she asked.

His voice was tense, "What do you know about Sabine? The inspector from Rome mentioned you. He said you were involved and that you had a drug problem."

"You were gone. I waited for you and you never came that night you were supposed to come to my place on via Gabbia but you never did, you never called, I had no number to call you and no place in Rome or anywhere to find you.

Then, one day, in the mail, came a certified envelope with a note inside and a certified bank check from a company I never heard of. The note only had a few words of love and goodbye."

"I had to do it. My wife, you must understand," he said somberly.

"Yes, of course, and thank you belatedly, Renato or should I say Armando; I am sorry I never thanked you for that generosity of years ago. I never saw you again to show my appreciation properly, as I was taught to do in boarding school in Britain," She laughed and moved to him, ran her hand around his neck, and kissed him then whispered, "Truth is, I have weaknesses too, darling, despite a very refined British education." Then she looked at him coldly, "What about the Sabine affair?"

He glared at her, "That's my question to you."

She fired back, "A girl needs security! Your check lasted a time but you know how I am and the cabaret is no vehicle for a showgirl's security. How long does that last? Although, I am proud that I have lasted as long as I have till now, and I am old enough now to be the young showgirls' mother. But I keep fit, that and genes and the fact I am blond and tall and have a nice bum. They like British showgirls with nice bums and firm breasts in Rome. But young showgirls, not middle age showgirls and I realized after you disappeared, I had a dim future approaching, despite my efforts to stay fit, age gains on a showgirl's body easily.

"Then Sabine's enterprise came in handy. It came in for a lot of the girls at the cabaret, which was a made to order recruitment center for Sabine, the young girls especially looked up to her because she had a headline act. Clever of her to use her influence with the girls, especially the young ones fresh from nowhere wanting the spotlight and the dream and always needing money and she was very flexible with the showgirls, realizing the attraction they had with her clients. It was all just a bit of naughtiness; all of the clients being refined with money to spend, randy and looking for fun! That's how she pitched it to me and I said why not. But now I've been sacked from the cabaret and things are very tight. And the Sabine affair has me afraid for my safety; leaving Rome with Gianni, a car was pursuing us…"

"Don't worry, it was the police for Gianni's protection and I can help you, of course, financially," Don Armando came to her and put his arm around her and asked softly, "Did you know about the undocumented under-age girls and Sabine's connection to sex and drug traffickers?"

"None of it! My connection to the enterprise was a telephone number, my payment in cash by clients."

"Did you know that she kept records of important names?"

Jill glared at him coldly, "Your name?"

He responded firmly, "Do you know if she kept records and files on the important and powerful clients she had?"

She studied him and saw him for the first time as a man without courage. "No!" her sharp response fell off into a silence that surrounded them with the unsettling loneliness of the night.

That evening, the Amalfi drive was a curved series of turns, masked by moonlight shadows that reached out from the sharp mountain rock, cut for a road to accommodate motorists and tourist busses interested in spectacular views of the sea coast. At night, the drive became an ominous threat to any driver unfamiliar with its character. But Gianni knew the road well, he knew that the moon would reflect off the sea and create optical illusions like the extension of the road beyond a curve that made it seem to link to the next curve, as if there were a straight road, instead of the cliff and a sharp drop to the sea below. That illusion had fooled him one-night walking with his friend, Ciano, when they were young. After a party and a few drinks, walking along the stretch of road just before Positano, he mistakenly followed the illumination reflected from the moonlight off the sea of the cove below that made it appear there was a straight road ahead. He was saved from a fall, when Ciano's hand grabbed his arm and pulled him away from the cliff edge that had been masked by the reflection of moonlight.

Remembering this, he drove more deliberately toward Salerno, mindful of the passenger in the car. He had learned to negotiate the Amalfi drive at high speeds, even in the late night with the skill of a racecar driver negotiating tight turns at a grand prix rally. He prided himself on his feel for driving the winding roadway with challenging curves that created blackout spots where nothing could be seen beyond the headlamps, giving the impression of being suspended into a dark void. But he knew how to downshift without braking and nudge the wheel to feel the road curve out toward the blackness of the sky that suspended at the edge of the cliff and if the moon were out, glide toward a shimmer of moonbeams as a guide out of the curve of the cove.

As he drove into a sharp curve, he felt the urge to accelerate coming out of the curve and allow the Maserati to drift more toward the edge of the road, where the cliff fell sharply from the road barrier to unsettle Paola, who sat tensely and hurled an invective "*Cretino*!" at him and looked at the road again, causing him to laugh as he accelerated along the straightaway.

The Maserati was a symbol to him, a reward for achievement and a sign that he had arrived as a professional in a special world dominated by celebrity. But beyond that, the white Gran Turismo was an aesthetic pleasure, the soft curves of the sport's design announced easy luxury with a whisper of elegance, unpretentious, but assured reinforcing his own nature, as he sank easily into the deep comfort of the driver's seat and held the wheel with the dexterity of a professional course driver.

The nightclub was packed as all the Italian dance clubs managed to be. This one in Salerno hid itself in a dark corner, a few yards from the large sea walk that wound around the beachfront that had received liberating American troops in the war. For Gianni, dance clubs were an annoyance; the crush of bodies was an assault, and the noise that claimed music, a confrontation. He had always viewed the young people who went to these places as 'drop-offs,' a term he invented to frame the figures that flocked to these places as children did to a playground after their parents dropped them off by car or released them from a pram.

Paola grabbed his hand and forced him into the scrum on the dance floor, wrapped her arms around his neck, and crushed her body against him in a forced gyration of hips and thighs. "You are off and not clever tonight, not being amusing for me. You said two words to me all night. I am being ignored, it seems."

“Paola, no man could ever ignore you, especially with this revealing tunic,” he remarked with irony and frustration over the annoyance of the loud music.

She pushed away from him and then pried her way to the bar. By the time he fought his way to her, she was already engaged in conversation with a tall man in a black velvet vest over a white shirt with half sleeves to air the tattoos on his arms. Gianni decided to move to the other end of the bar and order a brandy cocktail and then nursed it until Paola found him after she got tired of dancing and wanted to leave because she claimed that he was no fun.

She put on her blouse under the tunic, because of the early morning chill and fell off to sleep almost immediately after they drove away from the dance club. The convertible raced along a straight away and quickly gained the long climb to the Amalfi drive, when, suddenly, high beam headlights flashed like spotlights creating a blare of reflected light from the rear-view mirror, and flooded the interior of the car with light, just as it negotiated the sharp curve over the “new port” of Salerno. The beams gained on them quickly as both cars came out of the curve. Then the rear car came up to the side and tried to force the Maserati off the road, but Gianni slammed on the brakes, throwing the sleeping passenger forward, and awakening her as their car peeled off to the opposite lane, and then turned in the opposite direction and accelerated. But the pursuing car turned and raced after the Maserati.

Both cars raced along the winding road, the super charge of the white convertible achieving distance from the pursuing headlights for the first few moments, but the attacking vehicle made-up the distance at the next turn and again tried a sideswipe. But this time, Gianni was ready for it, and down shifted to cause his car to abruptly slow down as the other car flew on, and then he forced his car to touch the rear of the attacking car, which caused it to spin and crash its front end against a large mountain stone as the Maserati spun around and sped off in the other direction.

"Who was that!"? Paola leaned back in her seat and glared at him with the trembling look of a child awakened in fear from a bad dream.

"At first, I thought they were the police but that was not them," Gianni held the wheel tightly with both arms, stiff at eye-level for better control, remembering his training trials at Monza years ago, when he did a photo spread for a sports car magazine. He took the curves in the road ahead with a drift, releasing the gas pedal, then pressed it to the floor when in the straight away, gaining greater distance at extreme speed from the wreckage behind them.

He fell into silence, as did Paola, as fear separated them till they arrived at her home and she finally turned to him in anger, "Tell me everything or I shall scream and wake my mother and this town! I will not leave the car without you telling me! We could have been killed tonight. Tell me what is going on! Tell me what has happened to you."

"A showgirl murdered in Rome, who I knew, had secrets, dangerous secrets. Dangerous enough to have her killed and now the people who had her killed are after me because of those secrets."

He turned to her and saw fear in her eyes as she whispered, "The men in the car tonight."

He reached for her but she bolted from the car and disappeared behind the slamming *portone* door of her building, leaving the bag on the front passenger-side floor with the bunch of flowers and her string Bikini brief in it.

Gianni could not sleep that night after a shower and decided to shave and pack the small overnight he had. He waited for dawn then woke Jill and told her to pack and that it was urgent that they leave immediately. When he returned to the main-house, he was surprised to find his uncle taking breakfast on the *terrazzo* and he joined him and told him about the chase of the night before.

Don Armando studied his nephew's every word and then he spoke, "It's come to a bad stage, they have decided to take you out and make it appear an accident and cause the police to close the Sabine case. These men last night knew all about your movements. Therefore, you are not safe here. I will make some calls to Rome and get special witness protection for you. I think you should return to Rome immediately. There should be police protection for your place by the time you arrive. That is about all I can do for you now."

He knocked at the guest cabana and waited, then knocked again, and called inside, "Jill, it's Gianni, we have to leave now. I brought you coffee and croissant with marmalade." Jill opened the door wearing a towel. Her hair was wet from the shower. He stepped in quickly and laid the tray with the continental breakfast on the bed and turned to her, "I brought you something for breakfast. As soon as you're finished, we'll leave. I'll take the bags and equipment now and put them in the car. How long will you be?"

She looked at him as he went to the costumes case and stopped him, "I'll take care of the costumes and you care for the equipment. But why the rush?"

"Something happened last night that is connected to what happened at the studio in Pompeii and what happened to Sabine. It's best that we leave immediately and go to Rome. I'll explain everything in the car. My uncle sends his best and is sorry he can't say goodbye, he has important business to take care of."

"Yes, I would think so," Jill replied, as she went to the bathroom and prepared herself for the trip.

It was eight when they left the villa and the housekeeper closed the electronic gate behind the Maserati, which sped around the curve to reach the Amalfi drive. Gianni down shifted at the immediate sharp curve, then accelerated after shifting into third, and gained separation from the black Alfa that picked up his trail. Noticing the car, he became fearful that it meant to do him harm. He shifted into high gear and the sports car accelerated into a treacherous curve that wound along the cliffs, looming over a quick drop to the sea that only mountain goats scaled. But as his Maserati easily made each bank and softly drifted to negotiate the curve, he saw in the rear view, the Alfa keeping a safe pace at a distance and he relaxed and slowed down and continued the drive at normal speed.

"What were you doing driving like that?" Jill finally spoke, as she saw calm return to his face.

"Having fun with Rome's finest behind us for our protection but did nothing last night to protect me."

She turned and looked back and saw the black Alfa. Then, as she turned back again in the seat, her foot struck

Paola's bag. Picking it up, she fished out the bunch of flowers, noticing it, Gianni frowned, "They were meant for Paola but she had no use for them. Keep them for yourself or throw them out!"

Jill threw them out and then fished out Paola's string Bikini brief from the bag and held it up, "Shall I throw this out as well, since Paola evidently had no use for this either?"

Catch as Catch Can

The office used by the special unit investigating the Sabine case was an ornate remnant from another epoch, where the grand palazzo was built as a show of affluence and taste. The room was spacious with baroque fresco landscapes scaling the walls and scenes of the heavens inhabited by angels covering the ceiling around the labored fixture of a chandelier. Marco's slight frame was enveloped by the luxury of a leather executive chair, as he sat quietly at his desk, listening to one of two police officers standing before him.

The taller officer read from his report, "We followed from a distance because the subject driver used a narrow road in the outskirts of Salerno and was able to give us the slip for a time, but we were able to spot him on the Amalfi drive, as we recognized his taillights. He had a good lead on us when we observed a large car, which we were unable to describe make or model because of our distance. The car attempted to pass the subject's car, and as we proceeded on the curving road, we noticed that both vehicles were side-swiping that continued and broke off twice as they came to sharp curves on the Amalfi drive.

"There came a time when we could see nothing because of the night and a sharp curve. When we proceeded for a few hundred meters down the road, we came upon a sharp curve and upon entering it, our head beams revealed a car that had crashed into a large rock formation approximately fifty meters farther down the road. As we approached, our car beams picked up two men running across the road and then down the slopes of the mountain. We cut off the trailing operation and called for further instructions. We were told to contact the local police and catch up to the subject and if we could not do that, to wait at the villa where he was staying. We learned from the local police that the car that had crashed was stolen.

"At eight ten this morning, the subject drove off in his Maserati with a female from the villa and we followed, without incident, to Rome, where the car parked near 1102 Lungotevere at twelve seventeen this afternoon, and the subject and a female left the car and went to the above address. We left our surveillance of the subject at twelve fifty this afternoon after being notified by headquarters that the subject was under protection of the special security services and that we should make a report to this office at this time this evening," the tall officer looked up from his report.

The inspector sat up in his chair and placed both elbows on the ornate desk, "The escaping men were probably picked up by a backup vehicle, as is the case in a hit. How long have you both been in this department?"

"Five years, sir," the tall officer answered, "Three sir" came the response from the other.

The inspector stood up, "And with your training and experience, you were specifically assigned to do one thing and you could not do it, you could not tail a white Maserati on an open road in the hills outside Rome and then again on the Amalfi! Get out and tell my secretary that you are to be reassigned and leave the report with her."

He turned as they left and went to the large balcony doors on the other end of the room, opened them, and went out onto the balcony to smoke a cigarette.

He glanced down toward the Corso filled with cluttering headlights moving slowly along it, filling and jamming the feeding streets; starting from Piazza della Repubblica with its illuminated fountains that showered cars passing nearby as they rolled around as if in a circus ring and split off toward the train station or off to the side roads that led to the Tiber River and the old Trastevere quarter of the city.

To the aging inspector the scene represented the chaos of the city he grew up in. The heavy hum and blaring horns of moving traffic stymied his attempt at clearing his head. In frustration, he crushed the cigarette on the ornate balcony balustrade and returned into his office, went quickly to the door, opened it, and motioned for his assistant's attention, then commanded, "Get a car!"

From the rear police car window, the city streets were gauntlets with modern Romans cramming each other in cars, instead of chariots in a rush hour ritual. As a young boy, he remembered these same streets empty when the Nazis occupied the city. He recalled the ease of the post-war, when life returned to the streets and the future represented hope. In his growing youth, Rome was enlivened by the energy of freedom after the years of oppression from Fascism and the Nazi occupation only to stumble decades later into the malaise of corruption and political duplicity and the betrayal of the dream the end of the war promised. And now, he sat passively in the police car, looking at the Rome he no longer wished to understand pass by his window, knowing that he was part of a dysfunctional system generated from that betrayal and he was now in the process of protecting it.

The police car mounted the small sidewalk at the opening of the narrow street and drove up to the Cabaret Rome by Nite and stopped. The two inspectors left the car and went quickly into the cabaret as the doorman took off his cap and held the plate glass entrance door open for them. They walked quickly passed the vacant hostess station and into the salon, where a showgirl performed an erotic dance to a small crowd and then into the manager's office, without knocking, to find Elio behind his desk waiting for them. The inspector turned to his assistant and ordered, "Find the dancer Estelle backstage and bring her here," then he turned to Elio when the assistant left.

"Hello, Marco… It's been a long time," Elio stood up from his desk and moved toward the inspector with a smile, then gave him a hug, "How is my aunt?"

"Doing well, considering her age, she still laments the loss of her sister," Marco moved away from him.

"As I do, my mother was a suffering saint," Elio returned to his desk, took his silver cigarette case, and offered one to the inspector and apologized, "They are Turkish, not American, as you prefer."

The inspector waved off the offer, "Your mother, my aunt, was indeed a wonderful woman. It is because of your mother that I now find myself compromised. You being my cousin presented no real problem in the past; as a matter of fact, it was an asset, I have to admit, especially in the investigation of the Egyptian dancer who was involved with a terrorist sleeper cell in Rome. You have been invaluable to me before and to the GIS, the anti-terrorist police. We have looked away at some of your activities but now there is the Sabine case and the political intrigue fomenting around it and as recently as last night, an attempt in Salerno."

Elio sat behind his desk again and lit his cigarette, took a long drag, then looked up at his cousin, and exhaled, "Marco, I fully understand the situation but I am sure that the death of a showgirl has not ruffled the feathers of anyone in the police administration. But a black book has."

A knock at the door caused Elio to call out, "Come in," and the assistant inspector came in with Estelle. Marco motioned to her to sit at the sofa, which she did quickly, then announced, "Elio, you will have to leave!"

He waited until his cousin left and then faced the young showgirl, "Please, listen, we are here to get information from you concerning the death of Sabine de Ville. I felt it better to interview you here rather than create a media scene at my office. Be sure to answer my questions to the best of your ability and please be truthful. Any false statement from you now could put you into serious trouble with the police. Do you understand?"

Estelle looked at the assistant, sitting at a chair near the door, taking out a pad from his jacket, and then she looked at the inspector and replied solemnly, "Yes."

"It seems you are very close to your fellow dancer Jill, how long have you known her?"

"Has she done something wrong?" she asked in almost a whisper.

The inspector insisted, "Please, answer my question and remember to be truthful. I hope you understand the seriousness of the situation."

She looked at him for a moment with concern and then looked away as she answered, "I met her in Paris. I was a teen when I left home in Bristol to go to London to become a showgirl. I was good enough to make the chorus line at a small cabaret in London, but the pay was too little, so I decided to go to Paris to try out for the Crazy Horse and Lido where the pay was better and the chances for my career much greater. But I didn't make either of them. Then I met Jill at a party. We bonded immediately, both of us being English and showgirls. She got me into the chorus line at a small strip cabaret on the left bank. Then I developed my own feature act, which had success. Elio saw the act and gave me a contract to perform in his cabaret, here, in Rome, and I asked him to give Jill a contract because we were close friends and he obliged."

"Do you know about Sabine's background and how she came to work here?"

She studied the inspector for a moment and then her eyes wandered around the room as she tried to remember, "Sabine told me a story about herself some time ago, as I remember, she grew up in an orphanage in Toulon, France. She told me that Sabine was not her real name. The nuns who ran the orphanage registered her as Juillet for the month of July when she was found at the orphanage door one morning, baptized her, adding Marie as was the custom for female finds, and registered the appellation de Ville for 'from the city' to serve as her last name for the records. But she used Sabine as her stage name. She said she got the name from the scarf that was wrapped around her in the portable baby crib she was found in. It was her only link to family. It was silk and bore the illustration of a Roman fresco of semi-nude women being overwhelmed by Roman men with a Latin inscription that she managed to translate, when she took Latin at the orphanage's convent school, as the 'Rape of the Sabine Women.' She told me that Sister Teres, a young nun who mentored her when she was sixteen, referred to her Roman scarf and assumed her mother was from Rome and in a lapse moment of candor ventured that her mother was probably an Italian prostitute imported by the Mafia in Marseille to work the city's notorious waterfront and the Naval base at Toulon.

"Soon after, she left the convent school with the idea of creating an independent life using whatever advantage she could to make something of herself. She told me that to save money she hitched a ride to Marseilles to try to find her mother. She got a ride from a moving company van. The driver took an immediate liking to her and moved her into his flat. She immediately put aside all the virtues of chastity the nuns had preached and learned the value of promiscuity at sixteen. Fortunate for her, the driver was a drinker and a friend of the bar manager of a small cabaret strip club, which was near the apartment. She was tall and full breasted, thanks to her Italian mother, she was convinced, and when made-up she, looked convincingly mature and seductively attractive, so much so that the bar manager recommended her to the club manager. Evidently, one evening with the manager was convincing enough to put her in the topless chorus line. She claimed that she easily learned the necessary dance routines in the morning because she had ballet and dance classes at the orphanage and was in the line for the first evening's show at seven and in a short time, she developed her famous strip act and became a feature.

"But the money was never enough; the cabaret she worked in was just a seedy dump and not a place to develop a career. So, she resorted to a time-tested profession that her mother used and augmented her salary with an escort service. She never found a trace of her mother. It was a useless attempt to start with because she had no idea how to look for someone she had no description of or facts about. She met Elio who came to the cabaret and hooked up with him for one night. She said that he was so impressed with her that he offered twice the money to perform at his cabaret and gave her an apartment in Rome as well. She accepted on the spot. Rome being Rome, she soon found that *la dolce vita* was being an escort in Rome by night and not just a cabaret showgirl."

Estelle stopped speaking and looked at the inspector as an ironic smile came to his lips and then she observed, "Sabine viewed herself as a modern courtesan for the powerful politicians and the wealthy businessmen. In time, she organized what she called her own enterprise catering to them and she got the showgirls at the cabaret in on it one way or another."

The inspector interrupted, "Did you ever talk to Elio about what you have told me?"

She shrugged, “I don’t recall.”

“Was the apartment Elio gave her used for the escort business she operated?”

Estelle shifted in her seat and then said flatly, “Ask him!”

He glared at her, “How much were you involved in her escort business?”

She looked at him, “I would go to a party if a high flyer or a name was there and an extra girl was needed.” Then she smiled, “A girl likes a good party and to have fun.”

He leaned toward her, “You knew about a so-called black book!”

“No, but everyone knows now!” she protested.

“How friendly are you with the performer Annabelle Maritain?”

“Maritain?” she laughed, “Maritain, a French name right? Don’t hold to that name, according to Sabine, Annabelle is as much French as a camp follower is a virgin. And a camp follower Annabelle is!”

The inspector admitted, “She may have a picaresque history; we have her as probably Croatian.”

Estelle laughed again, “Gypsy, you mean, Gianni almost ran her down on a small road outside Naples one night. According to him, she ran in front of his Maserati, waving her arms, then leaped into the convertible before it stopped, leaned into him, grabbed his crotch, and placed a foot on the accelerator pedal to floor it, while screaming at him to get them out of there before those men who were running toward the car will beat them to death. Evidently, she rolled one of them, one of her own at that. And she’s been doing it non-stop to men, even now as respectable as she pretends to be as the not too discreet mistress of a deputy minister!"

The inspector raised a hand, "Please refrain from the gossip."

He turned to his assistant and waved a finger to strike the last remark from her, and then turned to her, and asked, "What do you know of Annabelle's relationship with Sabine?"

She shrugged, "You know probably more than I do."

He waved a hand at her, "Let's forget about what I know and tell me what you know."

The young showgirl shifted again in her seat, then smiled, "Annabelle latched onto Gianni and he used her as a model. He told me he was attracted by her bold attitude in front of the camera!"

She stopped to laugh at the phrase "bold attitude" and then continued, "Bitchy is more like it. He used her for a series he did for a French smut magazine and then for a spread on hard rockers for a London periodical, where he also used Sabine. The two hit it off, Annabelle spoke French because she had lived in Paris and in Marseille with waterfront gypsies and sang on the streets just like Piaf. She was deported with them to Serbia or Croatia by the French immigration as undesirables. She moved around with them for years and ended up in Naples, where she literally ran into Gianni in his precious white Maserati convertible."

Estelle paused again as an unpleasant thought changed her expression, "As I said before, he took up with her. Sabine got Annabelle a job as a performer here at the cabaret and enlisted her for her escort service until she met

Leonardo who is rich and in the government as a client, and her service was so good that she became his mistress."

The inspector turned to the recording officer, "Strike that, Carlo! You know what I mean. I think that is enough for now. Carlo, please leave us."

He waited for his assistant to leave, then announced in a threatening official voice, "You have false papers! They are good but false. Your story about working at the small cabaret in London is false. You ran away from a boarding school for delinquent children near London at fifteen. Sometime later you met Jill in Paris, where she befriended you. She helped you with the false papers because you were not of legal age in order to get you a job as a stripper in the small cabaret strip club Jill worked in. Then you both came to the Cabaret Rome by Nite. We know that Jill has a drug problem and that both of you have friends who are known to the police and that you both have done special things for Elio; special events that call for attractive blonds. And there is the additional problem that you were still under legal-age when you first came to work for Elio."

"I'm of age now!" Jill leaned back in her chair and then folded her arms in defiance.

"Yes!" he exclaimed in the voice of a cold inquisitor, "You still have the look of the innocent *ingénue* that perhaps serves you in your performances, and shall we say, special events. But it will not serve you to lie to the police. I can call in my assistant Carlo again and charge you with lying and false papers! Or you can start telling the truth now and I will forget all your misstatements and your false papers. Do you admit to what I said of your past?"

"Yes," she looked away from him.

"Were you under-age when you came to work at the Cabaret Rome by Nite?"

"Yes," her voice grew softer.

"Were you under-age when you started to attend Sabine's parties?"

"Yes," she admitted in a whisper.

"Good. Now everything you told me about Jill and Sabine, I have to take as questionable information from an unreliable source. I have no more questions now at this time but that could change. You may be very experienced for a young woman but please do not make the mistake of thinking you can outsmart the police. We are still looking into your past. Please do nothing to, in anyway, interfere or withhold evidence in this investigation and cooperate with us instead. Do not talk to anyone about what was said at this meeting. You may leave and tell Elio I want to see him."

She bolted from her seat and cried, "About time and I'll tell him you kept me here and delayed my preparation for my act."

She went to the door quickly and slammed it when she left.

Elio returned shortly after Estelle left and sat at his desk and listened calmly to his cousin.

"You understand my situation and how delicate it is with you my cousin being in the middle of this."

"I am not in the middle of the Sabine scandal, Marco!"

Marco listened to his cousin's voice and studied the expression of his eyes against the man and boy he knew. "In all our contacts, you never lied to me. Please don't now. This case is the biggest mess and most explosive media bomb to hit my office. These damn showgirls! Damn it, and you had a special relationship, shall I say, with Sabine, who worked here. The sordidness of it with the bordello and politicians, the media frenzy pushing the scandal. And the politics of it all! And last night, there was an attempt on the life of a principal in the case. It was a mafia-type attempt. Two men in a car, a 'drive-by' kind of thing gone wrong." He glared at his cousin.

Elio glared back, "I know nothing about what happened last night and I found out about Sabine's death from the news. It was I who fired her when the news broke about the scandal and I never saw her again."

Marco fired back, "You know people; underworld types who operate by night. The kind of people you could contact for a favor. It may not be a favor for you, but for someone you know who contacted you for the favor. Someone who you would be indebted to or who you would do the favor because it would be in your interest to do it."

Elio stood up, "I have done favors for many people, including you Marco. I did no favors for anyone last night! I realize your position with the Sabine scandal and there is no proof that I was involved with her business enterprise and the investigation must show it or I would have been arrested and you know that. But this much I know, from the people I know, you have a political bomb ready to explode in your face that could bring down this government. I am willing to help you anyway I can. You need me, my dear cousin, and that is why you are here tonight."

Payback

Drowsiness, then deep darkness and the sound of raw rock music, spotlights, a slim figure straddling a chair in front of a screen on a stage wearing an open black leather vest exposing her breasts; then standing and exploding in the kinetic energy of a dance downstage into strobe lights flashing her figure in neon patterns of color above the bar; the barman in a Marine t-shirt pouring a drink shouting, "She's one hell of a bitch. Save her for special gigs, like your return, Gianni!"

The stripper dancing into a soft blue neon flashing on her young figure; the music slowing to an isolated guitar to pose her in a quick defiant gesture, then leaning toward Gianni, peering directly at him, the light revealing her face with bright red lips, saying in Italian, "*Ti amo, caro*!"

The barman stepping between them, his eyes glaring and a solemn voice, "She's dead as dead as Joey. And we have a score to settle for him."

Fading to black, then waterfront streets, passing the car window, in ominous shadows from street lamps, the barman driving recklessly and speaking softly again, "The hit on Joey was a message to me from the boys who are backing the Colombians down here in the Hook and cutting into my turf. Tonight is time for payback for Joey."

The car moving into a long, poorly lit warehouse driveway, and then stopping…

The barman holding a pistol; the two walking down the dark driveway toward a large door…

Suddenly, shots ringing out…

Gianni awoke shouting, "Nino I'm hit!"

"You're okay, Gianni. Okay," Estelle whispered and bent over him and ran her hand through his hair as he looked up at her from the divan in his studio he had fallen asleep on waiting for her, "You were asleep when I came in and then suddenly, you began screaming about I don't know what. Something in your past, I think. You called out, 'Nino, I am hit.' Do you remember anything?"

He sat up and tried to clear his head as he focused on Estelle, who moved away to the costumes rack to take out a short black leather vest. "Is this the number for the urgent shoot you called me about last evening?" she turned quickly, pressing the vest against her body as he stood.

He looked at her for a second, and the black vest, "That's it. I just had a bad dream about it," then moved to the sink in the kitchen area, turned on the faucet, and splashed cold water on his face.

"Are you well?" she called to him after putting the costume back.

He did not reply, even after she came up behind him, she put her arms around his waist, and kissed his neck, "Poor, Nit, bad dreams again."

He turned around and embraced her, "Thanks for coming on short notice. I need an urgent additional shoot for a magazine assignment I did last week. You'll be perfect for it. It's time of the essence thing. This Sabine thing has interfered with work. Do you want coffee?"

"I'll make some!" she kissed him again and went to the cupboard took a tin out and prepared the coffee, as he went to the bathroom and washed. When he returned, coffee was set at the small kitchen table and Estelle stood at the window looking out at the river below "How awful to think of Sabine down there, ending up that way." She turned to him, "They pulled her from the water so close to this place, Gianni. Her death was a break for me though, sounds terrible, but my good luck on her bad. Elio has given me her act at the cabaret. Opening it tonight and I need you to come, please. Will you dear, Nit?"

"Of course." He took the cup of coffee from the table and went to the studio set up, placed the coffee cup at the design table off the set near the green screen backdrop, and then went quickly to set the camera on the tripod at the edge of background screen sheet that spread forward on the studio floor. "Let's get started," he called, without turning to Estelle and began adjusting the large format Leica camera for the shoot.

She moved away from the window and picked up the leather vest for the shoot from the costumes rack again then turned to the set and asked, "Am I to be in front of the green screen?"

"Yes," Gianni called back and went to adjust a light to the angle he wanted.

"What's the shoot for?"

"A hard rock magazine. I'll green screen images behind you. You wear the leather vest and make out you are dancing to rock music. I'll put on music to help the mood."

"This is just a vest, what do I wear with it? This Bikini brief?" she held up a hanger with Paola's brief on it.

Gianni turned, "No, not that. There are cut away jeans on a hanger on the rack. They'll fit you."

"Where is the top to the Bikini brief?" she asked, as she put it back on the rack, and then took the denim jeans.

"The owner has it."

"Won't she need the brief?"

"I'll bring it to her when I have time."

She began to take off her blouse; "You do have a strange relationship with your models, Nit."

He came to her to explain the costuming for the shoot, "No bra, keep the vest open to show enough to be provocative. The ripped cut away jeans will fit tightly on your bum. Keep the fly partially open and don't wear your brief for the randy. The leather boots are at the side of the dressing table, they're your size."

Estelle changed quickly and went onto the set, and suddenly a strong burst of light exploded onto the green screen set and rock music blared from a disk as she posed for the camera with strobe lights flashing while she moved testing one pose to another in sync to hard music.

Gianni began photographing but then stopped and called to her in frustration, "Be lively and more extension. I need more!"

Estelle attempted a few more poses but Gianni reacted negatively, and then she stopped and placed her hands on her hips, and glared at the camera, "I am doing a favor and would appreciate a bit of gratitude!"

"You have it from me but not from the camera lens."

"Camera lens!" She threw up her hands, turned to the set screen, ripped it down, and hurled it towards the camera, "This is for your damn camera lens! That's what I am to you just an image in the camera lens." Then she walked off the set, "You're like that bitch Sabine, no wonder the two of you got on so well. She was a witch of a lead dancer and chorus director at rehearsal. A perfectionist, like you, 'Extensions! Synchronization! Pose!' You'd think we were at the Moulin Rouge in Paris instead of Elio's dive on a forgettable backstreet in Rome where perverts and voyeurs share the same interest in boobs and bum for the cover and price of a drink at the bar."

She looked at him as he kicked the set screen to one side, "That's it, clean up the mess and worry about commissions for small change assignments to nowhere. Annabelle came to Sabine's enterprise and landed a rich and powerful winner and a large step up for her career ladder and dumped you because she felt you were a loser. Don't be a loser anymore, Gianni!"

She advanced toward him, "Sabine had names, lots of names of important clients, Gianni, all in her little black book with notations and other evidence safely hidden unless she had to reveal them. That's what all the showgirls are saying. And now Sabine is dead. She trusted you; all the girls at the cabaret knew she was tight with you, depended on you, calling you, receiving your messages. Sabine stuck to you, didn't she, Nit, even after it was over between the two of you. You know about the little black book, Gianni!

You hid it for her, didn't you!" She stopped speaking, placed an arm around his neck and kissed him.

He pushed her away, "Forget about it. Just call it a day!" And he started to clear the set again.

"Damn you!" she turned and walked toward the storage area, pulled the leather vest off when she reached the costumes rack, turned again and threw it at him. It hit his back and he turned to see her glare at him, then she moved her hips to the rock music, and pulled down the denim cut away jeans, as if she were in her strip act and smiled sensuously, then threw the cut away at him. In an instant he was on her, grabbed both of her arms, and pressing her hands together in an attempt to bring her to her knees

"What is it you want from me!" he shouted at her and then released his grip and stepped away as quickly as he had attacked her.

"We Gianni… We… It's time for us…now together, the two of us. That's what I want from you. I came here today not for the shoot but for us and what we can be together. We can have a future," she stepped deliberately toward him and folded her arms over her naked breasts and stood firmly in front of him as a nude interrogator, "Sabine's black book. Don't be a loser anymore; I know you have the black book. I know how we can make money from it. I have friends who know what to do with the names, Gianni."

He grabbed her wrists, "Friends? Maybe you mean the friend you might have been with in Pompeii who sacked my studio"

"What are you talking about? I know nothing about sacking your studio in Pompeii!" She pulled her wrists free and stepped back glaring at him, then slapped him and ran off to the dressing table, took off the leather boots, and threw them in his direction.

He advanced towards her, "What are you up to!" His voice exploded in the frustration of a man unable to unravel the danger that has taken over his life. "Who has gotten in your head?" he grabbed her by the shoulder. But she broke free with a quick twist of her body and went to the costumes rack and took a hanger as he advanced toward her.

She raised the hanger above her head and screamed, "Don't come at me again or I'll use this and scar the other side of your face! You are mad and a fool. You have a fortune in your grasp and you are a loser!"

He stopped and turned from her and moved away, as she ran to get her clothes and dressed quickly, took her bag and left, slamming the studio door behind her.

Later that morning, there was a knock at the door. When he answered, Jill entered and he gave her a kiss, "Thanks for coming on short notice."

She smiled, "A blow-up with Estelle then, how unusual!" She made her way to the dressing area and pulled off her pull over and then stripped off her jeans, paused to take a packet of cigarettes and lighter from a pocket of the jeans, and then threw the jeans over a chair, took out a cigarette and placed the packet on the nearby dressing table. She lit the cigarette and took a large drag, then exhaled the smoke toward Gianni, who came toward her as she placed the lighter down next to the packet, "Am I meant to be nude for this because I'll want the usual increase to show my lovely boobs but only for artistic imaging. I do have standards darling. And besides…I have reserves now…no longer desperate, you see. I came into some money and I've leased the old furnished flat I had near San Giovanni years ago. Stayed at the flat last night."

"The place comes with a friend or perhaps an uncle, I suppose," he said ironically.

"I can afford it for myself this time. But I still need to make a living and since Elio has banned me and Sabine's enterprise is closed, I have you and some resources and things look better. What am I to do then for this shoot?"

He pointed to the costumes rack in the dressing area, "I put the costumes for the shoot I started with Estelle there on the first four hangers. The jeans will fit you. You are the same size and body type as Estelle, and you can make yourself up to look like her. It should not be too much trouble. I'll pose you at angles and set lighting that no one will know the difference between the shots of both of you." He quickly returned to the set.

Jill went to the costume rack and sorted out some pieces and called to him as he was setting up additional lighting, "What do we start with?"

He called back without looking at her, "I need to finish the set with the leather vest. It's on the first hanger and the jeans under it."

Jill took the hanger with the vest and cut away jeans and noticed Paola's brief on a hanger. She took a final drag from her cigarette and threw it to the floor and stepped on it. Then she called back to Gianni, "This black bikini brief looks familiar!"

Part Two

Cabaret Rome by Nite

"... Always open to a good offer."

Elio the Egyptian, cabaret owner

The cabaret stage was dark, except for a single small spotlight at center stage when Gianni entered. As he went to the bar, guitar music rose and Estelle appeared with red and blue lights silhouetting her body. She was wearing a white mask illuminated by the small spotlight for the performance in a dance called "Mask." She began singing a phrase in a Gregorian chant with the stage mike making her voice echo, as if in an empty chapel.

The first word was "mask" sung as a lament in a piercing high note that silenced the cabaret and then a lower tone to the phrase 'love is a mask,' and then she danced classically in a modified ballet in bare feet. Her lean figure and long legs accented a series of kicks that suddenly broke the melodic chant into bump and grind runway music and brought cheers from males in the audience. The finale was a series of high kicks in cadence to blare drums with the stage lights slowly rising and showing her nude as she ripped off the mask to standing applause and bowed and then disappeared from view when the stage fell to black.

Gianni was finishing his brandy at the bar, when Estelle appeared at his side in a dressing robe, "I should just forget you and not even bother since you've been beastly but I am glad to see you've come to see my new act as you promised."

He shrugged, "I came tonight because Elio called and wanted to see me at this time. I see he's free now."

He turned to the barman and indicated he was moving to Elio's booth. When the barman recognized his gesture, Gianni turned back to her and whispered, "Come with me and say hello to him."

The cabaret owner was checking receipts, when he noticed the couple in front of him and smiled, "Ah, my American friend and Estelle, please sit. I see, Gianni, you did come in time to see Estelle's new act! Now she has two feature acts for us. She's a quick study. She did Sabine's act to perfection at first rehearsal and solved a major problem for the cabaret, substituting Sabine's age for the enticing figure of a young English blond was fortuitous. Blonds are always the most popular."

Estelle responded coldly, "I'd rather be thought of as a performer, Elio, as for my body, it seems that is simply what my men have only been interested in especially on camera. And I've decided to look to my future by myself."

Elio laughed, "And a great future you will have here, my dear. You had a problem with the black book, I understand…for the new act, I mean."

Estelle smiled, "It disappeared but we have a substitute for tonight."

"Where is the original one, Estelle?" Elio looked at Gianni.

"I am afraid that the original one is still missing." She made a move to stand and Gianni stood to let her out of the booth, "Now I should go and get ready for the new act and leave the two of you to talk."

The Egyptian looked at Gianni when he sat down again after Estelle left, "The usual?" and waved to the waitress who came over to the booth.

Gianni looked at the waitress, "The barman knows."

Elio interrupted "Tell the barman to kill Gianni's bill and bring what he is drinking." The waitress turned quickly and left.

"So, Elio, even Estelle becomes a part of this, and that is what you wanted to talk to me about."

The Egyptian took a cigarette from the silver cigarette case at his side and lit it with a lighter and then spoke quickly after taking a drag, "Two sinister looking men were seen backstage near the showgirls' dressing room last night and ran out the emergency exit when they saw the stage manager approach them. I fired the stagehand responsible for keeping the back-stage emergency-door unlocked after he admitted to doing it because the girls liked to hang around the alleyway for fresh air and a smoke. I told the stage manager to warn the showgirls that strange men were seen backstage. I think the men must know that you and Estelle are together and they came to find out about the black book. I know about what happened to you at Salerno. Estelle could end up like Sabine, you can see that, my friend. You don't want that and I don't want to lose another headliner for my cabaret. I told her the only way out was to cooperate with me and have you bring the book to me and then we could negotiate a way out of this mess for both of you."

Gianni asked forcefully, "Who are these men, describe them!"

Elio shrugged, "I did not see them and the stage manager got a poor look at them because they ran away. Things are unsettling around here now and it all concerns Sabine's black book."

Suddenly, loud bump and grind music caused Gianni to turn to the dance floor as the lights dimmed and a showgirl appeared, sporting a black top hat and white bow tie and a white vest covering her breasts, and wearing a black G-string. She moved sensually in spiked heels to the music, then stopped near a table where a couple sat, and tipped her top hat to them and her bow tie flew off onto the table. Then as the crowd laughed, she apologized to the couple and retrieved her tie and moved to the music again, until she stopped at another couple at a table and lifted her top hat as a greeting again, and her vest flew onto the table, when the audience exploded in laughter, the band sounded a runway tune to match the dancer's burlesque moves as she took her vest and moved off the dance floor waiving to the sound of applause.

"How do you know that there really is a black book, Elio?" the American whispered.

"That is what is going around."

Gianni insisted, "A lot has been going around, as you put it, lately."

They stopped talking when the waitress brought the drink. Gianni put a five Euro bill in her cleavage and she gave him a quick kiss and left quickly after noticing her boss's stern look for her indiscretion, "It is like play money for you am I not right, Gianni? Tipping freely around here. Estelle made comment that you spend freely but have few assignments and little work at the studio, and yet, you drive a Maserati Sport and go away for weeks at a time to fascinating and expensive places."

"I have a silent partner."

"Perhaps, someone in Brooklyn from your mysterious past or your influential and rich uncle in Naples?" the Egyptian leaned back in his seat, hoping for information.

"My partner is in Germany and no relative."

"Does he see a profit?"

"He has already realized a substantial one."

"I would like to know him," Elio smiled.

"Then he wouldn't be a silent partner, would he?" Gianni smiled back.

"You are a smart young man, Gianni, no fool but you play a fool's game with this whole matter!" the Egyptian stopped when the music suddenly blared again in a burlesque runway call. He motioned to Gianni to look at the stage, "It's Estelle doing the new version of Sabine's act."

The lights dimmed and images of numbers and names flashed on the stage screen. Gradually, a figure emerged from the projections and then a spot light on the figure's face, her blond hair up and wearing black rimmed glasses, then the spot widened to the full figure of Estelle wearing a short tight black skirt with a white blouse and black heels and holding a black book. A ring of the phone silenced the music, she turned to a desk, now visible by a second spot, then turned to the audience, and smiled and went to the phone, picked it up as the music rose again, and spoke, "Oh *ciao*...no...no! Madam is no longer available, *signore* Giorgio...*signore*, I mean...my honorable sir!"

The music punctuated Estelle's movements and her words, "Her little black book, yes, I have it here."

Estelle placed it on the desk and opened it with her free hand and turned the pages, "Yes, I see your page here with notations from the madam… Oh such notations make me blush! Yes, I will schedule you for tonight; I will be available for you…. *Ciao*, *signore* Giorgio!"

Estelle put the receiver on the phone and took a pen from the desk and wrote in the book, then turned to the audience as the music rose to a bump and grind, and she started to take off her blouse to the sound of the runway music and began the strip as numbers and names were projected on her body. The act ended with her wearing heels and black-rimmed glasses and numbers flashing strategically across her naked body while she smiled in a spotlight, "My honorable *signore* Giorgio. I am waiting!"

The stage went dark with a sound of strong applause from the crowd and a standing ovation. When the lights rose again, Estelle appeared in a white robe, took a bow, and accepted a bouquet of flowers and then disappeared behind the stage curtain.

"What was all that about, that wasn't Sabine's act?" Gianni protested.

The Egyptian whispered, "I call it the little black book act now."

Gianni leaned closer to Elio, "What are you trying to do with that act? Are the projected numbers real? Who is Giorgio?"

"Giorgio is the target, the numbers are numbers. It's a net, a fantasy… A trap. And you are in it as much as Giorgio is."

Suddenly, Estelle appeared in her dressing robe and Elio stopped speaking.

"There you are then, I've done 'me' act, boss, just as you planned it." She took Gianni's drink and drank it down and quickly placed it on the table again, tightened the sash around her robe, pushed Gianni into the booth, and plunked her taut sweating body beside him.

"My dear, you were seductive!" the Egyptian's eyes flashed as a hand tapped her wrist in support.

Gianni interrupted, "What's all this about with Sabine's act, Estelle?"

The showgirl fired back, "It's an act and a good one, I have a higher kick than Sabine and that makes it better, I did my hair up as she had it and basically the same movements…"

"Why the black book and the numbers?" Gianni interrupted.

"Ask Elio, he added that and changed things!" she sprang to her feet, "I can see you hated it, you think I am robbing from poor Sabine, don't you? Well it's my act now and I'll finally be the main feature here, the crowd loved it, you heard the audience applause. Everyone loved it but you!" She turned quickly and left.

Gianni glared at the Egyptian, "You called me today asking for a meeting at this time. You set me up for this. What is all this about?"

"It's a performance that I wanted you to see, and it has a message. And we have to see who gets it and then we can see what happens next in the mystery of the black book," the Egyptian smiled, "Bring it all to a dramatic climax, just like any good mystery! And when that happens, so comes the opportunity."

"The opportunity for what?"

"Treasure, Gianni! Whoever has that black book holds a great deal of damage to the present power system of this country and perhaps, other countries. Think of it… The damage to very important men, think of what they would do to stop the damage."

"You're talking blackmail, Elio!"

He grabbed Gianni's arm, "What blackmail… Just information sharing, a suggestion to the papers in a foreign country that gets picked up in the Rome media. No names but obvious important figures, an anonymous source speaks to an influential journalist… A major story is produced suggesting prominent figures are involved in the Sabine scandal. The T.V. picks it up and expands the story from anonymous sources with leaks from insiders with information, whistle blowers. Panic sets in among prominent people and contacts are made…compensations are made. You see how easy it is. How easy it would be for the person who had the black book and the person who had the contacts. It is all treasure, my dear friend, treasure. And there would be no more car incidents, Gianni."

The American stood, "You're talking about treasure we can't touch. The police are on me like hounds watching my every move. They are in here for sure right now. You know that. Why the show with Estelle? Are you wearing a wire? How did you know about the car incident in Salerno? I'm off and if there is a wire, say good night to them."

He turned away and left the cabaret. When he reached the outside, he caught the shadow of a figure moving quickly toward the end of the narrow side street, and then it disappeared around the corner. When he reached his car at the corner, he glanced around for a sign of danger and saw no one. He got in the convertible and drove down to the deserted Via Veneto, unwinding from the night crowds of tourists. Empty cafes were left to tired barmen and waiters alternating cleaning chores in the street side tables and shutting down the café bars that tourists from around the world flocked to in the hope of touching the magic of celebrities living *la dolce vita*.

The Maserati entered the Piazza Barberini. A black Alfa circled the baroque Trident fountain and drove behind his car, annoying him. He made a quick left and floored the gas pedal and the sports car flew down to the via Quirinale where it made a right and then raced at top speed to Piazza Venezia and for fun circled around the piazza in front of the white 'wedding cake' national monument, where two stragglers made their way across the piazza in trepidation of the two cars racing past them.

He drove flat out after that down to the river and onto Ponte Garibaldi and crossed over the Tiber and into the Trastevere quarter to race along the Lungotevere, shouldering the walls of the river banks to a small piazza where he left the car in the secure narrow parking space at the side of the small *café bar* his friend, Gaetano, owned. He locked the security chain and then walked deliberately to his studio. He paused at the palazzo's entrance and listened to the sound of the rapids breaking over the riverbed across the street below, where Sabine's body was found pinned at the embankment under the footbridge for the river island of Tiberina. He waited for the black Alfa to stop at the entrance of the footbridge and put out its lights while leaving its motor running. He turned and opened the door of the palazzo and went in and up the stairs to his studio.

Imaging

It was still early morning when he awoke and after a shower, he made coffee and had a croissant, then he checked the set cameras: the large format Leica for stills for the green screen inserts, and the studio broadcast video camera. Then he sat down at the Apple computer and brought up Final Cut and began viewing the unedited clips of Sabine as a Renaissance courtesan for the promo video for her script treatment of Rome by Night

The first clip was of her in a series of poses to set the feeling of a courtesan posing for a Renaissance artist. The next clip was a hand-held tracking shot of her moving in different nude poses in a confined space, where large canvases of nudes backed her figure. She managed the physical attitude of a Renaissance nude in her poses so convincingly that Gianni did a series of stills of her in various poses and used them to create a large montage photo print after the shoot.

The last clip was of Sabine in a cold monologue to the camera. "Rome by night, then and now, it is about women and money and the men who pay for sex. The courtesan was an attractive woman and that always has currency in Rome, as long as it lasts. But her men deserted her. She was alone out there left with nothing. So to survive, she took her talents to the street. Rome by night always awaits full of men with hungry appetites for beautiful courtesans then, escorts today, and since the Romans first built Rome and took the Sabine women.

"My little apartment now in Trastevere is over that filthy *Taverna Candida.* In the late nights, when the streets are still, the voices of drunken men rise from the floorboards and surround me in bed. I am always nude in bed and their voices caress my nakedness... Different voices of men, always men, and with their voices, come their smell rolling over my breasts, pressing my hips, separating my legs, and shifting my pubis, infiltrating me, moving my bum, pressing my thighs... Forcing me again and again, their breath suffocating me, punishing me, bruising me for more...more...endless more. And when I awake, I cry and I promise myself to get vengeance on all those prominent Romans who have now abandoned me and forced me into this life on the streets."

Lady in Black

The Cabaret was suffering from a limited Tuesday evening crowd as a trio played a tiring melody that attempted to soften the stale atmosphere between acts when Annabelle came to Elio's booth, reached for a Turkish brown from his cigarette case, and lit it with his gold lighter. After she took a drag and put the lighter down, she asked in French, "*Tout va bien?*"

He looked at her for a moment methodically, checking her performance costume, a long black gown with lace trim that allowed for a generous view of her breasts and a high cut from the hem to expose her leg to her G-string, "You are always in performance, 'The Lady in Black.'"

"You said you would handle it. Have you?"

"Complications, my dear. It seems your Gianni…"

"He is not my Gianni anymore."

"Perhaps, he should be again," the cabaret owner smiled

"What do you mean?" She took another drag from her cigarette.

"Gianni knows more than he says. I have seen men like him. He is more calculating than people give him credit for. And he knows how to use the connections he has. He plays stupid, claims he knows nothing, but he is the key to the mystery of Sabine's black book. You can get to him; you have that talent with men! Don't be a fool and lose the opportunity. Go to him and make a deal and we will have a fortune to divide."

He waited for her reaction and when none came, he changed the subject, "As I told you, I will be gone for a few days. You will handle the cabaret. Call me at Ostia if you need me. Now see if you can bring these stiffs to life with a song. The place is dying."

When the house lights died, a single spot came up to reveal Annabelle on stage in the black gown. Music rose with a Piaf like French torch song that she sang substituting sensuality for melancholy. She had what Elio recognized as stage-presence, with a certain danger about her that made her more an attractive diva and mystery woman for the male gaze to ponder than a singer with talent.

Gianni had told him about how Annabelle picked him up while three men were chasing her, because she rolled one of them for some cash and warned him about her gypsy background and her great capacity for inventing past events. But that only encouraged the Egyptian's sympathy and a protective attitude toward her, since he always felt an outsider in Europe himself. In a short time, Elio developed a close relationship with her; realizing that she had a great deal of street smarts that he could use to his benefit.

But the cabaret's feature performer had been Sabine who created a strip number based on a strip scene in Fellini's film '*La dolce vita.*' She was a look-alike of the actress who performed the strip on screen and the cabaret stage setting recreated the scene with a chorus dancer, cross-dressed in a black suit as the screen-actor, Marcello Mastroianni, accompanying her in the screen strip-scene.

Sabine was a genuine product from Fellini's world and audiences sensed it and her personal history confirmed it. The performance earned an opening night review from a number of Roman papers, and a semi-nude layout in men's magazines. A clip-on late night T.V. news generated an initial buzz of notoriety, which assured a standing audience, mainly composed of kinky males, a large number being Japanese on holiday or in Rome for business and looking for an erotic experience. As time wore on, however, Sabine's strip lost the interest of well-healed audience goers and the cabaret became a nesting spot of hangers on and sordid underworld figures, Euro trash types, and odd travelers suspended in the disquiet of Rome by night.

Elio's relationships to Annabelle and Sabine were conditioned by two factors; the first being the Cabaret, the second being Sabine's enterprise. He relied on Annabelle's ability to manage the entertainment while also being a feature performer and Sabine was indispensable as dance director and her feature performance had been the major attraction of the cabaret while her enterprise brought in money.

The cabaret also served Elio well as a front for various 'noir' activities that he became involved in. But now, the Sabine affair brought unwanted attention to him and scrutiny by the authorities that threatened to expose his 'noir' activities, which included his relationship with Sabine's enterprise. Such an enterprise could never survive without start-up money and a support system that had influence with authorities as well as the ability to provide protection, all, of which, Elio had and Sabine utilized at a steep price. He kept his distance from the enterprise and had no control over how she operated it. He was only concerned about the constant flow of cash that she generated for him. He never talked to her directly about it and could always claim he knew nothing about her escort business. He learned long ago the value of keeping quiet but with Sabine's death, nothing could be kept quiet. He decided to leave for his place on the beach near Ostia for a crucial meeting and leave Annabelle in-charge for a couple of days to handle the cabaret and the news media that had become an annoyance.

Elio's villa near Ostia was at a dead-end at the edge of a beach a few kilometers outside the town. It was a modest looking two-story white stucco villa with a generous balcony facing the beach and the sea. On the morning after he arrived, he had two visitors, who came in the same black Mercedes sedan. Leonardo was tall and lean with black wavy hair, without a sign of gray to reveal his fifty plus years, and wore an Armani ash, black suit and gray tie on an off-white shirt. The other visitor was Don Armando, his broad frame filled a tan sports jacket over an open-collar, light blue, monogrammed, summer, cotton shirt, and light tan, linen pants complemented casual tan loafers.

The Egyptian greeted them and took them to the balcony on the second floor that had a wide view of the sea and the rugged beachfront that was broken into isolated patches of sand between the rough of black pebbles and shards of slate and rocks. He made them drinks from the portable bar he prepared before they came and then sat down on a deck chair across from both of them, as they sat in lounge chairs that were separated by a small glass top table.

"As always, my friends, to your health and prosperity," the Egyptian raised the glass of gin and tonic and the others followed with their gin and tonics and they all took a drink. Then Elio placed his glass on a small table next to his chair and raised his right hand to wave at the panorama, "For us and the gods to hear and hopefully, there are no bugs to bother us."

Leonardo placed his drink on the table next to him, "I'm no fool and in no position to negotiate with the police and neither is Armando, so you need not worry about bugs. The question we have is about you, Elio!"

The Egyptian stood and went to the radio and disk player at the end of the portable bar, turned it on, and as Mina sang, he raised the audio, went back to his seat, and sat. "Mina…just in case others are listening too closely, despite what you say. So, then, what are your thoughts?"

Armando leaned forward and pointed a finger at him, "Everything is critical now and my nephew is at risk. I want your assurance that there will be no more nighttime car incidents. No more incidents period!"

Elio raised a hand to stop the accusations, "Don Armando, do you think I am so foolish as to jeopardize my connections and have anything to do with such a stupid and armature act. What could I gain from it? Your vengeance for sure!"

"The key is the black book," Leonardo stood and went to the balcony rail, looked at the sea, then turned, and glared at Elio, "The black book, Elio! Everything else is secondary. You and Sabine have collaborated for years, what did she have on you, only you and God know. Annabelle told me everything she knows and what Sabine told her…"

"How do you know she told you all she knows?" Armando interrupted.

Leonardo replied sharply, "As a lawyer, I evaluate information that is given and act on it. The rest is a matter of faith. From Annabelle, I know Sabine had a black book and she made all kinds of entries about her clients. That is the information I have. Are our names in the black book? It is speculation but none of us can afford to have that information in public, even if we are not in the book. For certain, it contains damaging information on our associates and friends that could lead to criminal charges, which, in turn, will damage us collaterally at the least. And that is not taking into consideration the aspect of moral scandals that would jeopardize the government and cause it to fall."

Don Armando waived a hand at the deputy minister, "Moral scandals…A standard of moral behavior in government? You are joking. Apply any kind of moral standard to politicians and you could never form a government!"

"Calm," Elio appealed, "At this point, we need calm. I have my contacts, as do both of you but mine are, shall we say, of a different kind. The information I get from them is that the incident near Salerno regarding Gianni was an attempt at kidnapping by people convinced that Gianni has the black book."

Armando glared at the Egyptian " Who were the men who tried to kidnap my nephew?"

Elio returned the glare, "I can assure you that when I find out, I will give you the names. I realize you are close to your nephew and with all my sincerest apologies, but I, myself, believe he is not being completely truthful when he says he doesn't know where the black book is. He spends freely as much as a wealthy businessman, yet my showgirls tell me that his studio is modest and he does not get that much work. I assumed that you were taking care of things for him but when I mentioned it to him, he said he has a silent partner in Germany."

Armando replied coldly, "I give him nothing other than modest gifts at times. He won't take money from me. He has never told me the details of the partnership, other than the German runs a large advertising company in Germany and he owed Gianni for an old favor and pays him back by having the German company finance his studio expenses and gives him assignments and contacts."

Elio turned to Leonardo and then back to Armando, "We have to think clearly. Let's look at Gianni without prejudice, Don Armando, I know about the questions that linger about him in Brooklyn, and out of respect for you, I will not go into them. But this strange financial benefit from this German partner, and with all due respect, I ask you both, is it not possible that Gianni may try and set up similar financial benefits by using the black book?"

Leonardo asked cautiously, "Armando, if that is true, what do we do?"

The Egyptian interrupted, "For me, the answer is obvious and it is Gianni. He is key to the black book!"

Armando responded angrily, "If any harm comes to him…"

"Who is talking about that?" Elio fired back, "You have the means, Armando, of convincing your nephew to work with us. You are the only one here who can. The incident on the Amalfi means he is in danger. There are others interested in the book and believe your nephew has it. And it is they who will do him harm. You can save him, Don Armando, convince him to work with us for his own safety."

Armando turned to Leonardo. "We don't know that he has the book and he is not the only suspect, to my eye, Annabelle is situated better than my nephew, she knew about everything that Sabine was doing."

"If Annabelle had the book, why would she use it against me! It makes no sense," Leonardo fired back.

Elio interrupted, "And why would she tell him and me that the book existed? She could have gone off on her own and used the contents, and don't forget she knew some of the clients personally and had no need of the book, if she wanted to blackmail them."

Armando turned away and was silent for a moment and then turned back to them, "I will arrange to see my nephew and handle the situation alone. I want no interference from you, Elio, or from your so-called contacts."

"Then the matter is in your hands," the Egyptian stood and went to the bar and offered his guests another round but they refused and decided to leave. After they had gone, he made a call from the house phone. On the other end was Annabelle, and after finding out the conditions at the cabaret, assured her that things were in hand and the 'problem' will be taken care of. After hanging up, he returned to the balcony, refreshed his drink, and sat down to look out at the sea as his thoughts focused on the next steps necessary to resolve the problem of the black book, without damaging any of his connections and himself.

The view of the sea brought his thoughts to the past. He was raised in Alexandria, the son of a Coptic Egyptian merchant and Italian mother. His youth was split into two cultures, the summers, and long school holidays in Rome with his mother at his grandparents' villa in the affluent Monte Mario section of the city, and the rest of the year in the European section of Alexandria. He had a disciplined education in a British school, which left a sour note about the British in his mind and about education in general. After his father's death, when Elio was a young man, his mother returned to live in Rome. But he decided to remain in Alexandria, where he quickly fell into lucrative black-market activities, until he was forced to leave and live in Rome because of the change in the Egyptian government and the crack down on underworld activity.

Rome was as hospitable to the underworld as was once Alexandria, where a young man using his wits, could forge a lucrative living on the edge of society. In Rome, the landscape changed but not the fast living and underworld activity. Elio eventually established the Cabaret Rome by Nite as a front to launder money. In time, however, the cabaret gave him respectability and a certain celebrity, when it became popular among the trendy Euro set. He enjoyed his popularity and as he grew older, gradually reduced his exposure to illegal activities. But he was still involved with Sabine's business and that presented a clear danger to him. A danger he would have to eliminate to save himself from the police.

But as he looked out at the panorama of the beach and sea, he felt tired and old, after hosting two old men, who, despite their age, conspired in a fantasy of youth. For Elio, the process of feeling old was a gradual one of losing something slowly and of things falling away, a loss of quickness and a fading alertness. As he pondered the course of action he might be forced to take, he realized he was no longer capable of making a cold decision, a sanguine one, one that could have fatal consequences. He had become soft and vulnerable and this realization had made him afraid. Being afraid was a thing he had always conditioned himself against. Being afraid meant that your wits were gone and you were no longer in control and ultimately, you were doomed.

As he continued to look out to the sea, he was overcome by melancholy. The sea before him at Ostia washed the delta of Alexandria and the freedom of his youth and he recalled the warmth the desert winds brought in winter, and the cleanness of the sky in spring, where the world seemed cleansed of sin and one could feel renewed. But now the sky over Ostia and nearby Rome had a different color as the day died and with it, his hope that he would do no more harm.

The black Mercedes made its way from the dead-end and onto the country road in the direction of Rome. For a long while, there was silence as Armando drove and Leonardo finished a cigarette and threw it from the car window and then spoke, "In the end, we have to deal with slime."

"I've soiled my hands before," the driver did not turn to him, "I have dealt with his kind before. They are never to be trusted. Protect your own my friend, as I will protect mine!"

Leonardo looked out the car window as it drove towards Rome and saw a landscape of cypress trees with scattered remains at clearings claiming witness to Ostia Antica, the ancient port that once served a proud empire. In his youth, he felt that he was part of that story, a continuance of that glorious history and culture. But that feeling had, long ago, left him. And on this day passing the remains of that glory, which now lay as unsettled ancient tombstone like stones and mortared bricks in fields at the edge of the sea, he was convinced that he was in Sabine's black book with notations about his sexual preferences that would bring him down and shake the government as well as his family name.

He was born with a title belonging to an aristocracy that no longer had claim to political power. A noble Tuscan family that could trace itself to the fourteenth century and the Renaissance in Florence, and even to the glory days of that Roman Empire that lay in ruins in the landscape passing the car window. The family made its first fortune as cloth and leather merchants and later as bankers and were active politically and competitors to the Medici family. Since that period, the expanded family retained title and influence in Tuscany and later in Rome in the twentieth century, when it was aligned with the King and then cooperative with the Fascists.

After receiving a law degree, Leonardo, dropped any use of title for political reasons and became a figure in the democratic government, where he served in various governmental offices, and was a current deputy minister in one of the agencies in the center left government; a position for all practical purposes of title with no protocol or function but one that would legitimize his presence in the government.

Although he had been separated from his wife for years, the scandal would prompt her to bring divorce action against him and win a major financial settlement. He was facing personal dishonor and a ruin, as final as the ancient ruins of Ostia Antica scattered in the fields passing the car window, if the black book were not found and destroyed.

Gianni opened his studio door, answering a small rapid knock, and found his uncle. The visit was not unexpected and as the two sat on the divan in the living area, Gianni listened intently to his uncle, who spoke with unease in his voice after he finished the glass of red wine offered by his nephew, "Rome was always a special place for me. An escape from Naples as my business grew…and as you well know, in the nightlife. Jill was a part of it; I am not revealing anything to you. I am sure of that, Gianni."

He stopped speaking for a second to see the affirmation in his nephew's eyes and then continued, "We met at a party given by a 'big' in the government. I don't have to tell you that she is an attractive woman. She charmed me and we had a relationship that lasted for a time. It is painful to tell you this and I know how much you love your aunt but you must understand that she is the reason I broke my relationship with Jill. And I will do anything to keep her from knowing about all of this. You probably already realize that my indiscretions were not limited to Jill and implicate me in the Sabine affair."

Gianni leaned toward his uncle in a gesture of comfort and asked softly, "How deeply?"

His uncle's eyes reflected an appreciation of his nephew's concern, "Deep enough that if there is a political scandal, I could be ruined. All politics is a swamp, your Brooklyn, as you well experienced and Rome, which has ironically ensnarled us both deeply in a political scandal involving women we both had relationships with…"

Gianni interrupted, "Are you now paying for an apartment for Jill?"

His uncle shook his head and said, "No… How could I now with all this going on!"

His nephew pressed him, "In the time of your relationship with her, did you notice anything that brought suspicion to you? Anyone who you might have suspicions about? Someone you met when you were with her who she knew?"

Don Armando sat back and glared at his nephew, "I avoided being seen with anyone when I was with her, that's why I paid for a place for her near San Giovanni. Where are you going with this? Forget about Jill; think about getting out of your problem with the police! I can help you do that but you must be honest with me about everything!"

His nephew spoke in frustration, "Everything? The black book is what you mean!"

His uncle stood and glared down at his nephew, "If I get the black book and not the police or the media or the underworld, I could change things for you with my connections!"

Gianni exploded, "I don't have the black book! And even if you had it, that won't exonerate me of Sabine's murder, even with your connections. The police need the murderer to close the case and they have already decided on me. Don't you see? Listen to me! I need your help with the investigators, I've thought this out. The murderer has to be found and it's not me!"

A Matter of Taste

Leonardo realized that the family name was at great risk. He had lived with the pride of its birthright and gifted by the inheritance of title, even in Italy's chaotic democracy, title held respect and meant privilege, allowance, comfort, and immunity from the socialist chaos that overwhelmed Italy in the post war years. The family estate was solvent in Tuscany, the lands were safe, and the businesses flourished, the family yacht, the place in Forte dei Marmi, the villa in Prato, all safe. The apartment in Rome was the government's perk and his till he left office; this and the government stipend and pension would be his financial loss. What was at risk was the family name being dragged into a scandal that could explode into the media at any moment and with it dishonor to the family name and criminal charges against him and a ruining divorce.

When he arrived at Annabelle's apartment, she was still in a black silk nightgown at the bedroom dressing table, fixing her face for the night's performances. She had finished the bottle of Prosecco on the table, next to the empty wine glass sitting in the disorder of make-up spread on the tabletop.

"So, then, where are we?" she asked when she looked away from the dresser mirror.

Leonardo ignored the question and picked up the wine bottle and saw that it was empty, "Should you be drinking so much? You have to perform tonight."

"Wine relaxes me, enriches the imagination, and makes me fly through performances and helps me to forget the losses in the day," she looked down at the make-up and then started again to make her face, "And you are avoiding my question."

"There is nothing to say, there was no meeting. Do you understand?"

"Yes," came in a whisper as her eyes looked in the mirror and saw him moving out of the bedroom with the empty bottle.

He threw the bottle into the wastebasket in the kitchen, then went to the bar in the large costly decorated living room, and took the open bottle of Remy Martin brandy and poured a full glass. He sat at the large sofa and took a drink, then placed the glass at the lamp table at the end of the sofa. He looked around the living space, at the curtains drawn over the window, then at the bar, and the radio and player in the lavish wood console and felt that everything was slipping away. He was a stranger to all of this now, even to Annabelle. The passion he always felt for her had vanished when he saw her at the dressing table. She had become an element, a character in a drama that would consume him.

His mind shifted to his youth and his many dalliances with women. He was Catholic but not religious. His Catholicism was a formality that came with his title, status, and family upbringing. He thought of the religion as an accessory to his aristocratic class, a thing to be demonstrated as a matter of taste, like a silk tie on formal occasions or at church ceremonies. He never read the Bible and his mind always wandered in sermons when he had to attend mass as a formality. He was convinced there was a God. A punishing but forgiving one, the God of Michelangelo on the ceiling of the Sistine Chapel was the example and the Christ of the Last Judgment was His son. In the end, religious art became esthetic images rather than religious ones. Morality was negotiable and situational and his dealings with women followed that notion. He married as an obligation to family. She was from an aristocratic family but the marriage fell apart with a separation after a few years and no heir to the family title and fortune. But that duty was left to his younger brother and sister.

Approaching sixty, he suddenly felt old and burdened by the weight of past dalliances, poor judgment, gambling losses, business misadventures, and the time wasted on frivolities, trips, meetings, assignations, and sexual indiscretions culminating in the Sabine affair. He, long ago, realized his vulnerability, when it came to sex and his taste for attractive young women, who were younger and younger as time went on and, in the end, too young. Now he faced criminal charges and prison, if Sabine's black book reached the authorities. His only hope was Elio and Annabelle who came and sat next to him and passed a hand through his still dark hair and rephrased her question from before, "What could have happened at the meeting that never happened?"

He studied her eyes and saw again the calculating spirit she always had, "You lived with Gianni. He is the key to everything. You know him. You know how to handle him. Go to him. Get to him and get the black book from him!" He squeezed her left hand in his right.

That next morning Rome had a crisp wind from the hills that cleared the early heaviness of the night air. It was Saturday and Rome slept longer to leave the streets clear of traffic and allow the morning to have its way along the Lungotevere river drive that brought her to Gianni's studio.

He was having breakfast when the door to the studio opened and Annabelle walked in with the key in hand. "You never collected the spare key and I kept it and you never changed the lock," she smiled, closed the door, and came in and then sat across from him, "I am not surprised. You knew I would come back one day, didn't you? I have left before and always came back. And do you know why?"

A slow ironic smile came to her lips and he knew she was playing again, "We are the same, Gianni, I knew that from the first time we met when I rudely jumped into your car. Anybody different would have thrown me out or drove to a secluded place and raped me. But you did neither. And I knew then that we could be safe together and we started a good relationship for a time, no? So, I felt bad about our last meeting and thought I would come to apologize for so rudely accusing you of killing Sabine."

She studied him as he stood up, went to the sink with his empty coffee cup and plate, and put them down. Then he turned and came to her, picked her up, and they kissed.

She put on her slip as she left the bed and went to grab a cigarette from the pack of French Gauloises she left on the kitchen table. After she lit it, she moved over to the set, and looked at the Leica camera on the tripod, fiddled with it and managed to turn it on, and then hit the replay and looked at the photos in the display screen. Gianni followed her movements from the edge of the bed and when she noticed him, finished her cigarette, and put it out by crushing it on the tripod out of habit, "Estelle looks different in the last photo I've just looked at."

He slipped on his pants and came to her with a curious look in his eye, shifted the camera, and looked into the replay screen as she leaned into him. He viewed the photo. After a few seconds he announced, "That's not Estelle, that's Jill. She finished the shoot after Estelle bolted out in a rage. They do look alike, don't they? Unfortunately, I can't use any of it. Thanks to Estelle. And I have a deadline to meet!"

Annabelle looked into the screen again and shrugged. As she turned to him, she kissed him, "Always problems with your women, Gianni."

Then she moved away to the dressing area, knowing that his eyes were following her every movement. She stood in front of the dresser mirror and studied her figure and then ran her hand over her breasts. "Still a firm appealing figure, even now at my age. No sagging breasts either." Her eyes were on Gianni appearing in the dresser mirror.

"Still a youthful look." A slight smile made her glance ironic, "It is important is it not, firm breasts and fine figure? Keeping a lady young, no? Helps to keep me employed as a performer, an appealing cleavage can help the song, you see."

She paused and her eyes wandered, as the light from the dressing area window caught the high arch of her cheek in a cold tone of alabaster white. "The miscarriage, here in

Rome, when we were together, back then, spared the fine form. Unintended benefits," her voice rippled lightly in a dark corner of the studio and then she glared in the mirror at him and shrugged, "Meant to be, no? Should not stay depressed about it, should I? I should be thankful, no? Am able to model for you again as well, if you want Gianni... Still a muse to your camera's eye, no?"

She turned from the dressing table and came to him, "I have gained not a single kilogram since we parted," she ran both hands over her hips. "Women hate fat on their hips but not a millimeter added to mine, no flab and firm breasts. I am as slim as when we first met as you can see," she rested an arm on his shoulder and her lips were firm in a cold kiss.

Then her eyes flashed at him as she stepped away, "I would never have lost the baby if we had not been here in Rome and were in New York instead," her voice strained, "New York would have saved our baby."

She moved away from him and recovered a natural tone of voice, "I cannot blame you though, with your troubles in Brooklyn, pity for me hooking up with the only American who cannot go home again. Seems the Mob is at your heels back there, a sharp guy like you living by night in Brooklyn with Mob problems, how unusual."

Her laugh was ironic and her eyes enjoyed the stir that those words brought to him, "Don't be angry darling you live by night as I did being 'Rom.' Like Piaf, I had a voice and I lived as she did by night with the underworld and sang with gypsies on the streets of unfriendly European cities and then performing in the cheap cafés and trashy cabarets. We know each other, Gianni, because we come from the same world. We belong together."

He studied her as she moved to the studio-set again and turned to him, "Gianni, we can start again. Work together again, too. You said you have a deadline now; I can work with you as I have done before. I saw the costumes for the shoot and they fit me. We can work together; you and me, as it was back before the bad times."

"And Leonardo?"

"It is over."

"Why?"

"I am tired of old men."

"And his money?"

"He is lucky to avoid jail. He is implicated in the Sabine scandal," she waved a hand casually to make the point.

"You met him at Sabine's enterprise."

She became silent for a moment as he came to her and studied him again to see if what she would say would win him over, then she confessed, "Yes, you were away on assignments, I became lonely after the miscarriage and would go to Sabine's place occasionally as a friend and one time I met him. He was very kind and attentive."

"I bet he was and the money wasn't bad either."

She embraced him, "I hurt you I understand and I was wrong to do what I did. We should not make a mistake again, Gianni."

He broke from her embrace, "Who sent you here, Leonardo or was it the Egyptian?"

She focused her eyes coldly on him, "No one sends me!"

"Your right!" he smiled at the falseness of her indignation. "Exactly right, no one ever can send you. No one can control you, not even the gypsies, back when we literally ran into each other for the first time. And I can't control you now, I never could."

When Annabelle returned to her apartment, she found Leonardo on the phone. She went to the bedroom and got undressed and took a shower and afterwards, put on a bathrobe and sat at the dressing table and began the basic makeup she needed for the cabaret performances. She always added the eyelashes and final shadow just before performing in the cabaret dressing room. She had just cleansed her face with a face wash and added a basic foundation for her makeup when he came to her.

He touched her shoulder gently and she looked up and he asked, "So, then, does the plan work?"

She added touches of makeup and then turned to him, "In the years with him, I never trusted him to tell me the truth."

The Cabaret was full on a Friday night. Elio had returned from Ostia and was pleasantly surprised by a full booking, thanks to some special events happening in the city, but he also felt the notoriety building in the media about Sabine and her being a showgirl at the Cabaret Rome by Nite contributed. He went to the dressing room and found Annabelle adjusting the straps to her revealing black gown for her performance, "You look very beautiful tonight. There is a full house for both shows. Evidently, publicity, bad or good, is always good for business."

She looked at him coldly in the mirror as she sat at the dressing table and fixed black eyelashes to her eyelids, "Good for cabaret business and bad for us, if we don't settle this thing about the black book. I was with Gianni today, I don't trust him but I am sure he has the book," she whispered so that Estelle and two other showgirls, who were talking to each other at the other end of the dressing room, would not hear, "You have to sort things out with Leonardo."

Elio glanced at the other showgirls and then back at her, "We can talk later after your performance."

He left the dressing room and spent some time backstage with the crew and then went into his office. He was finishing up some paper work of the cabaret expenses when there was a knock at the door and after he called to come in, Estelle appeared in costume for the last act of the first show.

She held the glasses for the act in her hand and sat down to adjust them and tested the proper fitting to her face, "Annabelle is being bitchy in the dressing room and apparently, she is back as an item in Gianni's life. She saw some modeling takes of me at his studio today and made cold comments just now, while smoking her French cigarettes that only a French whore or a gypsy tramp like her would smoke! She slept with him."

"Did Annabelle say that?"

"She doesn't have to."

"Perhaps, then, Annabelle brings back a past love to him," Elio sat back and a smile came to his face.

"There you are looking smug! And what am I to do now with this situation with Annabelle?" she fitted the glasses in frustration.

"I think you are over-reacting, he still has an affection for you, I am sure, play on that. This thing with Annabelle will play out and we will make a decision when things are clearer. Now, you have your act and I have bills to pay," the

Egyptian stood up and escorted her to the door, and then asked, "Did you know the two men who were chased from backstage a few days ago?"

Estelle studied him for a moment, then answered with a question, "And if I did?"

The white Maserati flew into an empty Piazza San Giovanni in the late night. He saw in the rear-view mirror that the police tail followed at a distance as he drove passed one of the arches of the old wall. Then, suddenly, a black Fiat came across from his right and tried to cut him off. He swerved to the left, down shifted, and mounted the empty sidewalk, then pushed the accelerator to the floor, and shifted into high gear to ride down the street with the Fiat driving after him. He turned left at an intersection and accelerated till he came onto the tight *piazza*, where the Fiat cut him off again and tried to force him against a large wall. But he managed to avoid the Fiat and escaped down a side street that led to the Basilica San Giovanni, where the Fiat chased him, until, suddenly, the black Alfa of the tailing police appeared and sped after the Fiat, chasing it down a side turn-off.

When he arrived at the apartment near San Giovanni, Jill was waiting for him, "You look flushed darling, a hard time tonight?" She wore a comfortable white housedress with a revealing low cut.

"A chase again. The police came in time and hopefully, got them." He kissed her on the cheek.

She embraced him, "Are you alright, darling?"

He shrugged, "Right now, I'm just glad I'm here in a safe space."

"Sit and relax!" she led him to a sofa near a large draped window that overlooked the side street of Via Gabbia and they sat together.

"Why did you want to see me tonight? You sounded agitated on the phone. What is happening? Here take some chilled white wine I put out for you." Jill took the wine bottle from the ice-bucket on the coffee table in front of the sofa and filled two glasses. He took one and drank and then placed the glass on the coffee table and looked cautiously at her.

"The black book does not exist," he stopped speaking and studied her expression. Jill's eyes fixed on his as she frowned in an expression of confusion when he announced, "There was never a black book."

"Then what the hell is all this about?"

"Sabine invented it!" he looked into her eyes.

"How do you know that?"

"She said so on this," he lifted a chain form his neck and showed a Flash drive hanging from it, "She recorded herself and made the statement about the black book, claiming she invented everything in order to protect herself. Then she said the videos on the Flash drive are more powerful than any black book could be. She narrates a series of videos from what must be surveillance cameras she hid in different parts of the bordello she ran. The videos and her narrative are as devastating as any black book!"

"How did you get this?" Jill touched the Flash drive.

"I was looking for a book late this afternoon in my studio, when, by accident, another book fell from the bookshelf. The book that fell has a leather jacket similar to what the Renaissance books were bound in. When it fell, a secret compartment twitched open and the Flash drive was in it. The book was Sabine's. It is a book about Renaissance courtesans that she used for the script we were developing. There is enough on the Flash drive to send a lot of important people to jail."

"What are you going to do with the Flash drive?" Jill took a drink of wine and studied him closely.

"I don't know."

"Will you take it to the police?" she asked after she put down the wine glass.

"I can't," he replied firmly.

"Why?" her voice was pensive.

"If I brought it to the police, they will still think I was part of it. They know about my relationship with Sabine. They will only think I was bringing it to them to make them think I didn't kill her, but they are convinced I did. And then the police will recognize the important men in the videos and the names listed in PDF files. And everything will go to the higher-ups, who will want to suppress it and get the Sabine affair resolved quickly and get it out of the media! My arrest would do that and take the pressure off, and they would seal the case file with the Flash drive in it as evidence for trial, effectively putting an end to the bad publicity, which is exactly what they want to do. It's Rome and you know, as well as I do, Jill, about Rome."

"Then what are you going to do?" She stood and moved toward the window.

"I have to find the killer and that alone will get me out of this. When you see what is on the Flash drive, you'll understand why."

He inserted the flash drive into Jill's lap top computer, opened a video file, and the voices of girls were heard off camera in a foreign language, perhaps Romanian, then two young teen girls who were probably Rom, the appellation given to clandestine gypsies by the Italian authorities, moved separately into view in a wide shot of a room with the only light coming from a small lamp on the corner table. An obviously under-age teen moved to a dark corner, glaring nervously as another teen girl moved near a draped window and began stripping in front of an older man sitting in a chair. When she finished stripping, the man stood and took her out of the room with him. The screen went dark and the clip ended.

"That man was Leonardo! Annabelle's companion!" Jill called out. Then Gianni opened a file named client fourteen. It contained a PDF document titled 'C' containing a list of female first names and their young ages listed with dates and payment amounts. Then, he opened the file with the title 'Cara.' It had a PDF document with pictures of a young, teen girl nude and comments about her physical features and what sexual services she will perform with cost amounts.

"Shut it off, Gianni, please! It disgusts me. Is your uncle in a video?" Jill asked coldly.

"His name is on a contact list. That's all I could find about him. But it's enough. Sabine knew what she was doing. She left the book at my place saying that we can use it later. She wanted me to access the files, if she couldn't."

He took the Flash drive from the computer and re-attached it to the chain and placed the chain around his neck.

Jill took the laptop from the coffee-table and shut it down, and then took it to the shelf by the window where she kept it, and turned to him, "What are you going to do now?"

He stood and came to her, "It's evidence that could be used to find out who killed Sabine. But I can't bring it to the police, as I said before, because they'd still think I was involved with her operation and maybe her murder. The only thing I can do is to try and find out who killed her."

He turned away and went to the coffee table and took the bottle of white wine, filled his glass, took a drink, and then reflected, "Sabine was tortured by a form of water boarding; she had plain water in her lungs and was dead before she was thrown into the Tiber. Elio got that information from his contacts at police headquarters. She might have mentioned my name when she was being tortured and maybe about the book with the Flash drive hidden in the leather cover and they came after us in Salerno. They could not get to my studio in Rome, because they knew I was under surveillance by the police and did not want to risk a break-in. But they got a tip that Sabine left some things in my studio in Pompeii and they went there to search it for Sabine's black book or the Flash drive, if they found out about the Flash drive from her. But they found nothing and have been trying to get me ever since, including tonight."

"Who gave them the tip about your studio in Pompeii?" Jill came to him.

Gianni moved away again, "I told a lie and found the truth."

"Who did you tell the lie to?"

"Someone I trusted," he replied

"Someone I know?" she came to him and touched his shoulder and as he turned to her, she asked, "Was it your uncle?"

"No."

"Who was it then?"

"Estelle," he studied her eyes as they moved nervously away from his gaze and measured her silence and then he asked, "What do you really know about Estelle?"

Jill looked back at him and then she spoke deliberately, "Met her in Paris, she was young then and under-age, treated her like a sister and helped her with false papers to get a job at the cabaret I was working at. You know all that."

He pressed, "Yes, what I want to know about is her relationship with Elio."

She studied Gianni's expression and the frank look in his eyes then she spoke coldly, "She is a tart, you know. Plays the game of *ingénue* quite well, manages you by being endearing, cuddly, and darling to you. I've seen that act before with other men, many men before. I suspect she is playing the same darling game with Elio as well. But knowing him, he'll play along, as long as it suits his purpose. Estelle is me, just sixteen years younger, but she has a colder heart. You see, I had family and wasn't sent away by my mother as she was. She'll never know her father. She was put in a boarding school at six under his name. Her mother couldn't have her around and take care of her because of the odd hours and traveling on the road in a burlesque strip show moving around England. That kind of life leaves no space for bringing up a child. There were rare visits to the boarding school but letters and postcards were regular. Then came an opportunity in Paris and mother went off."

Suddenly, the apartment door opened and Estelle came in. Jill looked at the figure at the door and announced, "Estelle was her grandmother's name. She has a rebellious side that one-day, at fifteen, landed her in a reformatory because she ran off with a bloke and they broke into a shop and stole money to get them to London. Six months later, she managed to run away from the reformatory and came to Paris to meet her mother."

"You!" Gianni glared at her and then at Estelle advancing from the door.

"Yes. I called her after you called me and told her to come after she finished her act," Jill looked at him and then turned to Estelle, "It's all on a Flash drive. He has it on a chain around his neck."

"Give it to me then," Estelle demanded and came close to him and took a small pistol from her sweater pocket and pointed it at his chest.

He reacted by pushing Jill into her daughter. Then, in one quick upper-cut thrust, grabbed the gun, but it went off firing a bullet into the ceiling as both women fell to the floor. He twisted the gun out of Estelle's hand and pointed it at both of them and called out, "Who killed Sabine?"

"I didn't kill her!" Estelle shouted back as she came to her feet and helped her mother. Then suddenly multiple police sirens sounded and flickering red lights lit up the drapes covering the window and disorienting the women.

Gianni looked at Jill, who looked back at him with despair, "Sorry, Jill. I've been working with the police with the help of my uncle," he flipped the collar on his shirt and showed a small bulge where a small microphone was stitched into the fabric, "Technology today is a marvel. The police were listening to your story, sorry."

The heavy cadence of rushing feet that sounded from the hall-stairwell silenced him and he went to the door and threw it open to find a squad of policemen in assault gear filling the stairwell and the floor landing.

After four assault officers entered the apartment to surround the two women, Marco came in, stood at Gianni's side, and formally addressed the stunned women. "I am charging both of you with conspiring to tamper with evidence in a murder case and using a weapon in the process of committing that crime. We have arrested two men who tried to kidnap and harm a witness in the murder case tonight. They are also being held as suspects in the murder of Juillet De Ville, known also as Sabine. Both of you are also being charged with being accomplices to her murder."

Both women were handcuffed by two policemen and led away without saying a word.

Gianni followed Marco to a street corner, away from the police cars, and the confusion of police and mingling on lookers and announced, "We have a deal," and offered the Flash drive to the inspector, who suddenly placed a finger on his lips and reached over to the American, turned his shirt collar, and ripped out the concealed microphone, threw it to the pavement, and stepped on it, then picked it up again.

"Pity it broke," he said coldly, then he took the Flash drive from Gianni, and placed it in his pocket, turned and went over to a black Mercedes sedan parked across the street with its motor idling, leaned into the open driver window to have a few words with the driver, then reached into his pocket and handed the driver the Flash drive. As soon as he stepped away, the driver window went up and the car sped away and he returned to Gianni and smiled, "We have been working all night on this, while you had a drink with Jill."

"The black Mercedes has the Flash drive," Gianni protested.

"What Flash drive?" the inspector smiled and pinched the American's cheek as his car came up and stopped next to them. He immediately opened the rear door and sat and then asked the driver, "Carlo did you see a black Mercedes?"

"No, sir," came the immediate reply from the driver.

The inspector smiled at Gianni, "Stop making up stories for your own sake and for the good of your family and give my best to Don Armando when you see him again. You will remember, won't you?"

The car sped off when the inspector closed the door.

The Eternal City

The city of Rome was created by the grit and cunning of a group of family clans and from that city, an empire grew. The empire lasted as long as the grit of those families lasted and when that vanished, so did the empire, but the city of Rome survived even after conquests and defeat. It survived because it never lost the cunning of its founders. The cunning endures as strong as the ancient stones of the Forum to make the Eternal City the city where anything has always been possible, and the sinister details carried out in Rome by night.

He left the Maserati at the usual spot and walked up the narrow side street following the glow of the neon of "Cabaret Rome by Nite." When he reached the cabaret door, the tall doorman opened it, giving Gianni a long look. When he entered the cabaret, he passed quickly by the bar, avoiding the barman's look and didn't bother looking at the semi-nude showgirls doing an improvised act to fill Estelle's act for a sparse audience. When he got to Elio's office, he knocked and went in, when invited to and sat down at the desk across from the Egyptian, who never stopped glaring at the American until he settled into a frustrated voice, "You are a fool. You had everything in your hands. You had Rome by the balls. Jill and Estelle were used as pawns by the two 'Rom,' who were so incompetently trying to kidnap you. They set up Jill in her apartment. She had a habit and was desperate for money after I fired her. The 'Rom' idiots gave her money and the apartment and all the coke she needed in order to get you and your uncle."

The cabaret owner shrugged, "Estelle was working with them and managing the clandestine, young girls and using Sabine's place. Poor Sabine probably did not know what Estelle was doing until it was too late."

The Egyptian shook his head, "Then the scandal and the rumor of a black book and the 'Rom' idiots kidnapped Sabine and killed her by using American water boarding technique to maximum ineptness," Elio raised his hand in disgust, "And Annabelle has disappeared because she is a 'Rom' herself and I think could be implicated by the two incompetents the police caught. Sabine is dead, Estelle in jail, and Annabelle on the run. And I have no headliners for my cabaret. You have seen the nearly empty room. I had all the showgirls go topless for every act, even the female performers that I hired to substitute for Annabelle and Estelle and still no crowd, I don't think having them perform nude will mean anything!

"With that flash drive we could have had the Eternal City and the government in our pocket, if you would have listened to me. Instead it is buried in a restricted file in the special investigations unit," the Egyptian stood and went to the small bar near the bathroom door, poured two brandies, turned, and went to the American and handed him a glass, "Remy Martin cognac, the only thing we ever agreed on."

"What is your exposure in all of this?" Gianni asked, as he took the glass of brandy and watched Elio return to his seat behind the desk.

"You always ask the wrong questions, my young friend," Elio smiled then drank the brandy and watched as Gianni finished his glass, "One thing about you has been pressing on my mind and I know it is a violation of privacy that I always respect out of necessity, especially in my, let's say, profession. But I am going to violate that principle and ask you about your silent backer. I would like to know about him. One can always use a silent backer. I can go through you, if need be."

The American shook his head and smiled softly as he put down his empty glass, "Not possible. You see, I have a unique agreement the result of an event that almost cost me my life."

The Egyptian leaned back in his chair, "Now you have captivated my interest, my friend. Tell me more."

Gianni smiled and settled back in his chair, "No real names or addresses… Let me say a fiction, you understand that."

"Of course," Elio waved a hand in compliance.

"Five years ago," Gianni thought again, "A little more than that, but it doesn't matter."

The Egyptian shrugged.

"I was on the run, you know that I had a problem on the Brooklyn waterfront where I got this scar."

The cabaret owner moved his head in agreement as Gianni touched his scar and continued to speak, "I backed into a problem with some wise guys and they were out to get me. But I slipped away, thanks to help from some people. I ended up in the Caribbean. I was in a club off the beach on a small island keeping away from things, when a German blond, who I had met, came up to me at the bar and said she wanted to dance. We danced and she got friendly. What I didn't know was that she had run away from her husband in Germany with a lot of his cash but he caught up with her that night. He was rich and an owner of a big German corporation. He paid investigators to track her down; that's how he found her. She was living with a guy on the island but he busted up with her. I didn't know any of this that night while I had her in my arms dancing with her. Suddenly, her husband appeared and pointed a Luger at me to show how much he did not care for me holding his wife. My instincts took hold and me being very gun shy after my Brooklyn experience, I took off and he ran after me. He fired the Luger twice, when he couldn't catch me, as I ran down a dark alley and missed, but I dove at the sound of the gunshots and struck my head on the porch-post of a house owned by the local constable, who flew out his front door at the sound of gunfire with his service revolver in hand. I was out cold and when I woke up in the local clinic, my head was bandaged. The blow from the porch post got me on my old gunshot wound and the doctor assumed that the wound was a graze from one of the shots from the Luger.

"While I was still in the clinic recovering, a lawyer showed up representing the German millionaire. He explained that his client mistook me for the man who ran away with his wife and that his client was extremely regretful about the incident and any harm he had caused me. A couple of days later I signed a police statement saying that no bullets hit me and the bloody wound was an old one that opened when I struck the porch after I fell because I was drunk. I claimed I had no knowledge about the reason for gunshots."

Elio leaned forward with interest, "And the German's end of the agreement?"

"Investment in my studio and a large line of credit."

"With a forgiveness clause, of course."

"Of course, with certain limits."

"And the problem in Brooklyn?" a concern came to Elio's face.

"Settled a couple of years ago."

"Wonderful, my friend!" a broad amicable smile came to the Egyptian's lips as he stood, "Thank you for that story, which reinforced my faith in you. But now I have to go and try to make this place profitable again. So, you will excuse me."

As both men reached the door, the Egyptian put a friendly hand on his guest's shoulder, "As much as I regret the lost opportunity of us doing business on Sabine's list of names, I respect the fact that you saved some very nervous heads, famous heads indeed, including a very personal one to you; a noble thing preserving family honor, if not a profitable thing. The loss of profit potential always angers me, but honor has currency, even in this corrupt eternal city of Rome, and debts do have many ways of being repaid that a clever man with family connections could take advantage of. Perhaps, a more cooperative relationship between us could develop in the future, especially, if by chance, you come across a copy of Sabine's files or the originals, my friend. I can always work with a clever man who has connections. I vented a bit just before and apologize and am glad you came to see me. It shows respect and that is what I have always seen in you. We can always talk and as you know, I am always open to a good offer."

The memory of the Eternal City escaped in the rear-view mirror, as the white convertible ran along the Appian Way, through idle fields marked by cohorts of aged and angular cypress trees regimented toward the past horizon of empire and glory. The sun was an eternal mentor warming the speed of the Maserati negotiating the southern lane of the road that once directed ancient legions to create civilization beyond the plains and hills of Lazio.

It was just afternoon when Gianni drove the car past Sant' Agata sui Due Golfi and down the winding curves that entered the Amalfi coast and one o'clock, when the gate of the villa in Positano opened, and he parked the car by the passage that went past the garden and swimming pool to the villa, where his uncle was waiting to greet him.

They sat for a lunch prepared by the housekeeper on the *terrazzo*, as the afternoon filled with a warm breeze from the sea. Don Armando poured a second glass of chilled white Soave and refreshed his nephew's glass, "Drink and eat more. You have to be more philosophical about events and not brood. There are always casualties. Managing them is always a goal. I have it on good information the English showgirls will cooperate with justice and receive minimal sentences and then deported as undesirables. The 'Rom' assassins will be dealt with harshly. It makes for favorable media, given how much the public hates their kind. But I want to talk to you about the future. I am getting old. I have no son to help me out. You know that and my offer to come on board is still there. Paola is working with the firm part-time and doing wonderfully. But she is a woman and young and a student. The firm needs a young man like you. I need you both, Gianni. You and Paola could make a fine pair. You both are family and that is the most important thing. In Italy family always survives. Everything else is transient."

The late afternoon sun mellowed in a haze of tan orange and settled beyond the mountain cliffs of Santa Maria del Castello above Positano, as the Maserati chased the fading light at the edge of the cliffs till it rested in the field that ended the road. He took the small wood box from behind the driver's seat and walked to the edge of the cliff and looked out at the sea shrouded with the evening haze and then the shoreline of rolling hills that ended at the water's edge to create the Amalfi coast. He slid open the cover of the box that resembled a miniature coffin, reached out over the edge of the cliff, and emptied Sabine's ashes into the wind that scattered them toward the sea and then let the box fall.

He remembered Sabine's words and whispered, "Now, you are free and timeless." He said a payer and ended it with "God rest her soul" and then turned quickly to go to his car, when he saw a black Fiat Spider race through the curve down the road and then come up behind his car and stop. He walked deliberately to his car, reached into the passenger seat, and pulled out Paola's black bikini brief. Then he turned to see the Spider's driver's door open and Paola jump out from behind the wheel dressed in an easy white shift that clung to the youthful trimness of her frame as she walked up to him briskly.

He smiled and greeted her with, "Ciao, cousin, this is yours," and held up the brief.

She took off her dark glasses with her left hand and then slapped him with her right, causing the bikini brief he held to fall to the ground. Then she embraced him calling out, "We are not cousins!" and kissed him.

Printed in the USA
CPSIA information can be obtained
at www.ICGtesting.com
LVHW010815051023
760202LV00003B/126

9 781643 786636